I0831252

The Music Festival

By: B.L. Lacarski

Published by B&J Lacarski Publishing
3214 Maple St, Erie, PA 16508
BJLacarskiPublishing@gmsil.com
Visit our website at bjlacarskipublishing.com

Library of Congress Control Number: 2023903770

First Hardcover Edition: March 2023

ISBN: 979-8-218-14909-3 (Hardcover)

Dedicated to Jennifer

Happy 30th Birthday!

Table of Contents

PREFACE

Preface Song:

"The Only Difference Between Martyrdom and Suicide is Press Coverage" by Panic! At The Disco

The following story is one that is told as the first edition of a multi-part series. This series contains dual-authorship between B.L. Lacarski, and J.A. Lacarski of B&J Lacarski Publishing.

This series is unique in that readers have the opportunity to enjoy the novel on a deeper level, stimulating the senses to better immerse the mind into the plot. This is done through music. Each chapter comes with a song suggestion for you to listen to. It's designed to add more depth to what is going on in the book, or the overall theme of that part of the story. Because of this, you might find the chapters are relatively short. This is in part to better align with the length of a song, and also to divide the story up by mood or theme, and move on to the next moment with a new chapter and a new song.

You can enjoy the music while playing it along while you read, or feel free to listen to the music first to get a sense of the mood of the story, or listen to the music last, to help fill in the blanks or understand the meaning on a deeper level. I encourage all listeners to purchase the music by the original artists in your favorite form for listening to music (digital, vinyl, CD, tape, etc.) Spotify subscribers can enjoy these songs on the B&J Lacarski Publishing Spotify Profile. A curated playlist is designed to compliment each novel in this book series.

There are many different ways readers can use the music as a tool to add imagery, depth, and emotion to the novel.

I crafted this book specifically with the average adult in mind. My hope is that it appeals to the general masses who want to sit down and enjoy a quick, exciting story. Because of this, I chose specifically to omit any dense vocabulary or description that many non-readers tend to skip over anyway. It is a book that should flow naturally with regular human thought processes and dialogue, without taking away the richness a novel brings.

Please note: despite its simple vocabulary, shorter chapters, and larger font, this book is not for children! It contains adult subjects and content intended for a mature audience.

This first edition of The Music Festival series was a true delight to write. I hope you as a reader find it just as enjoyable to read.

CHAPTER 1

Chapter Song:

"Hungry Like The Wolf" by Duran Duran

"There's something in the barrels of water, and frankly, I'm a bit terrified," I said to Melissa.

"Jelena, I think you're overreacting. The heat is getting to you, and Brendolyn's crazy theories are clearly forming a colony in your head," Melissa replied. She loves fantasy, but makes a clear distinction between it, and reality; or what she perceives as reality. Lately, I haven't been so sure.

"Fine. Don't believe me, but I'm telling you, people are turning into werewolves, and I don't want to be next. I'm not drinking that water."

"Okay. Well, you're going to dehydrate if you don't, so why don't I just boil it for you? It'll kill whatever werewolf morphing bacteria that's in it, so you can stay human."

I'm still reluctant, but hesitantly agreed. Melissa is stubborn and is just looking out for me. Plus I really do need to drink something. I haven't hydrated enough in days; not since the second day of this crazed music festival, when this monster shit all began.

"And Brendolyn's theories are not crazy! She's making a lot of sense!" I defended her. I'll admit it was delayed. I process things slowly sometimes, like my brain computes on dial-up. Melissa is used to it though. She is also tired and getting over my shit, so she just rolls her eyes and continues in her effort in starting a fire to boil the water. Which is about to taste disgusting being warmer than piss, but whatever. I'll drink mud at this point. I'm so damn thirsty.

Brendolyn, the crazy woman of subject, who also goes by Dolly, is off doing who knows what; probably some earthy, mystical, hippy shit. I don't know. I can never keep up. She's my wife, and I love her; platonically. We're not actually married. It's more like the vows of a marriage. We are eternally devoted and committed to each other's well being. We've been under this marriage agreement for years. It really works for us. As far as romance goes, yeah, there's none of that. Hell we don't even live in the same town or see each other more than maybe twice a year. But we've been friends for ages. Possibly even quite literally if you buy into all that reincarnation hogwash. I don't know what I believe. I don't dismiss the theory, but at the same time, I'd like to see more concrete evidence that it's a real thing.

Melissa on the other hand is my twin without being related. We share a birthday, have similar interests, and really hit it off in college when we were dorm neighbors and discovered we hate cohabiting with strangers and had our own private rooms. She can be a bit unreasonable at times, but she's cool for the most part. Plus, she's looking out for me in this desolate apocalyptic music festival we're living in.

"Here. It's hot, but it's clean. Drink it." Melissa brings me a bowl of piping hot bubbling water. Fortunately we brought camping supplies with us. Otherwise, we'd be really fucked. The costs are jacked higher than ever for this festival. People are going ape shit like the 1999 Woodstock festival, only this time, instead of Limp Bizkit and angry horny men setting the place on fire, it's being overrun by horny emo fur beasts who keep the rest of us up all night while they howl at the silver glowing sphere in the sky. I guess werewolves are some type of canine species. So they probably think it's just a ball they want to play fetch with. I don't know. All I know is something sketchy is going on here, and I thought werewolves were just for thirsty Team Jacob obsessed 'Twilight' nerds and not actually a problem I'd be encountering any time in my life. Yet, here we are. And here I am, parched and suspicious of drinking our only water supply left; the rain barrels of stagnant water sitting out like watering holes for the animals that we all are, trapped here at this music festival.

Although, despite all the chaos, the music is still FUCKING AWESOME! So we stay. I don't even know if we're trapped here or not. No one seems to even be trying to leave. Now that's how you know you're at a good ass show.

"Are you going to drink it, or just peer into it blowing ripples while you drool?" Melissa asked, kind of snarky.

"I've been show-shing it, thank you very much! I'm not trying to burn my esophagus here."

"Okay, well it's been like 15 minutes now. I don't think it's going to cool down any more. Especially considering this heat we're sitting in."

Had it really been 15 minutes already? Not a chance! Or has it? I don't know. I have no sense of time anymore. Everyone's phones are dead or out of service. The sun is hotter than blistering balls on Satan's scrotum.

I drank the water. It was gross. Then I threw it up.

"Lena, I know you're thirsty, but next time, maybe don't chug it," Melissa said to me.

"Shut up, I tried."

"I'm just saying, it sits heavy in an empty stomach. Plus we have to conserve what we have. It takes 20 minutes to boil the werewolf turning bacteria away," Melissa reminds me.

That reminds me. The werewolves. We're infested with them. "Don't you think Brendolyn's been gone for too long?" I asked. I'm starting to get nervous.

"What? You don't think she's been turned, do you?"

"No. I don't think. I don't, how should I know? I've never been in this situation before. We don't even know how people are turning into werewolves to begin with."

"Well, maybe she's just enjoying the festival. Who's on the main stage now? Bowling for Soup?"

I shrug. Again, no sense of time over here. And the map is long lost.

The next thing I know I'm on the ground feeling like I've been hit by a train. I'm pretty sure my body is crushed to bits, but the adrenaline is holding it all together. Because out of fucking nowhere, Brendolyn (who DOES NOT RUN, even for a corn dog) plowed into me and yanked my arm out of its socket while yelling at Melissa and me to run. So I run. Because if I don't, I'll be dragged.

"Why are we running? Where are we going?" I ask.

"Wolfies! Just run!" Brendolyn says. She's out of breath, and that's all she can get out. Well, if it wasn't fucking obvious, these beasts aren't something we want to be messing with. I don't even want to know what triggered them to start a stampede headed for our campsite.

"Where's Melissa?" Brendolyn asks.

"What? I don't know. She was running with us, wasn't she?" I could have sworn she was running right alongside us. *Where'd she go? Did she fall and get hurt? Did she take a shortcut? We're far ahead of the pack enough, I don't think they had her surrounded and gobbled her to bits…. Did they? No. No, that didn't happen. We would have heard the murderous blood curdling screams. Which I didn't hear; or did I? No. I didn't. Damn this heat sure doesn't help me make sense of what's going on.* "I'm sure she's fine. She probably just ran into a different direction. We'll have to look for her later when it's safer. She probably found a place to hide out for now," I reason.

Finally we find a place to hide until the wolf men pass through. We hid in silence, quietly catching our breath. This is not the ideal situation for people to be so exhausted to be in. I need a fucking nap. But who can even sleep when the place is being overrun by wild animals?

"Where have you been? What happened? And what happened to your face?!" Brendolyn had been gone for a long time, I know that much. And when she came back, she was being chased by the beasts, and now that we've slowed down and caught our breath, I see that she has a gash on the side of her face that's bleeding.

"I was listening to the bands play. And I found a small stage with a really good band that no one was paying attention to, so I walked over to listen. And I don't know. The lead singer had sparkling sapphires for eyes…. Like, literal SAPPHIRES! Not just a line to say they were blue and sparkly. And then next thing I know, I'm being vag-y rammed doggy-style, and when I finally look to see who it is, it's the new ringleader of the human-dogs. I gasped, and it pawed at my face, cutting my cheek with its claws. So I ran. Then I heard it howl, and well, angry wolf mob, and here we are," she explains.

Nothing surprises me anymore. "So how did you go from listening to rhinestone eyes, to being raped by a beast?"

"I don't know. It was like a cut scene. I don't know what happened."

"Did you drink anything? Or eat anything?"

"No. I don't trust this shit. I think that's how people are being turned into the creatures."

"Okay. So we're all either delusional, contact high as fuck, or something really fucked up is going on here. Either way, we need to find something we can trust to eat. Otherwise, we're puppy chow."

"Okay, well, what can we eat?"

"The fuck do I know?! I drank hot piss water and puked it up before you jump-started my heart and made me run ten miles."

"You drank the water?!" Brendolyn is very concerned about the water.

"Yes. But Melissa boiled the bacteria out of it first, so we should be good," I reassured her. I am not about to be the next hungry wolf. I'm just hungry. Hungry, hungry, human.

"Okay, but if you start feeling a little dog-y, let me know," she cautioned.

"I will. But I do think I'm fine… anyways, where can we find food and hide out until the next show?"

Brendolyn looks around and ponders for a bit. We have to be very careful we don't draw attention to the dogs. I suspect Alpha took a liking to Dolly's scent. Now it's locked in, and the pack is out for their prey… us.

"Ok, let's go through the woods and circle back to our campsite. I think I have some emergency snacks stashed away."

"YOU HAVE SNACKS?! I THOUGHT WE WERE OUT OF EVERYTHING!"

"Calm down Miss Hangry! They're EMERGENCY snacks! I always have emergency snacks. They're probably stale, but I'm sure it'll do. At least for now."

She was right. This hunger and heat is starting to get to me. I gotta get a grip.

"Okay. Let's go find these snacks."

As we stealthily make our way back to our campsite, I replay the whole week of this festival in my head. *How did we even get here?*

CHAPTER 2

Chapter Song:

"Festival Song" by Good Charlotte

******Day 1 of the Music Festival******

"Okay, I have snacks, cash, noise canceling earbuds, sun screen, and a big ass baggy full of drugs," I said while packing my bag into Brendolyn's electric green Jeep. The drugs aren't the fun kind. It's more of the survival kind. Prescription strength Tylenol, Aleve, Excedrin, Pepto Bismol, Tums, Vertigo meds, ADHD meds, you know, the ones we will need to take to stay sane during this week long music festival.

"Great! I have the directions preloaded and studied, I have the playlist, gas in the car, money for tolls, more snacks, blankets, pillows, chairs, foot cream, and just about everything that came in travel size at Target! Oh and mini bottles of booze!"

Brendolyn is always prepared too. She can be a little nutty and forgetful, but she tries, and she always has a plan. And she packs way too much! I've known her for over 25 years. It's never changed.

"And I have cases of water, I baked cupcakes, I have body glitter, practical shoes, band-aids, tissues, toilet paper, camping supplies, and ponchos in case it rains." Melissa is always thinking about the little things that we might not think of, like ponchos.

"Good call on the ponchos. Cookware! Let me ask my dad where the cast iron skillet is, and if I can borrow it for the trip."

"Yes! Perfect for self defense!" Brendolyn chimed in.

"Or for making pancakes and moon pies." Melissa corrected her.

"Yeah, that too. But you never know when you need to give someone a beat down. I watched 'Tangled' you know," said Brendolyn. She's not wrong. Self defense is important at these kinds of shindigs.

Once we got the car all packed up, we said our goodbyes to my family, and we were off! Heading on the road with snacks and a killer playlist that was meticulously crafted to get us amped up for the music festival. It's a classic rock meets emo/punk fest, like Warped Tour meets Woodstock. It's the first one ever, and it's about to be legendary. All the best artists from our generation, older generations, and even some younger ones will be represented. Music is very much an important part of our lives and a core pillar to our friendships. So it’s just obvious we weren’t going to miss this.

It was a long drive, so on the way there we caught up on our lives, laughed, told stories, snacked, took naps, all the things you look forward to on a road trip. Plus we’re all pretty chill, so no drama!

Before I knew it, we were there. I had to piss Like a motherfucker, and of course there were only porta pots in the parking lot, and a big ass line at the gate to get into the venue.

"I'm holding it. I'll go in the woods before I use one of those nasty things." Brendolyn took one look at the temporary waste infested restroom and made up her mind real quick. She's always been a bit of a germaphobe.

"Well I can't hold it, so that's why you hover. I'll be right back." I ran off to do my business and when I came back to the car, Melissa welcomed me with hand sanitizer. Thank the Lord!

"Okay, are we ready friends?! Leggo!" That's Brendolyns's way of saying 'let's go'. She can be way too chipper sometimes. It's the cheerleader in her. I don't know why she does it. Can you picture an emo cheerleader? She's All dressed in black and gray with heavy eyeliner and black nail polish, and then jumps around with pom poms with the biggest smile on her face. And she genuinely loves it too. But who am I to judge? It's who she is. And she's good at it; or at least she was. We're all past the age of agile athleticism these days. We're likely too old to be going to the music festival as it is. We're not super old, but we're also not spring chickens either. We're your typical millennial.

We made our way to the big long line at the gate to have our bags checked at security, and find our spot to set up camp. It's about 11 a.m. at this point, and the sun is already blistering hot. I'm wondering if we even packed enough sunscreen and water.

Just as I was beginning to regret my choices, I felt the impact of a tackle and I just about took a bitch out with self defense. Some guy out of fucking no where just ran right into me.

"Yo! Watch it! Save that shit for the mosh pit bro!" I yelled in aggravation.

"Ah! Sorry! I'm color blind and didn't see you there! My name's Borris by the way." A shaggy-hiared tall 20 something year old said with a sheepish "nice guy" smile I was seeing right through. I wasn't sure if I should call out his lame excuse of a pick-up line or laugh at the fact that he's the victim of cruel parents who named him Borris. He can’t control his lame name, so I chose the former option.

"Color-blindness doesn’t make me invisible. Try again."

I could hear Brendolyn snickering, and I could feel the excited look of thrill in her eyes to see where this new entertaining romcom will go. I have news for her, it’s about to go straight to the back of the line!

"Oh. Yeah. I guess not, huh. Well, it worked on the last girl."

"Well, I’m sorry to say it, Borris, but maybe you should raise your standards and try approaching smarter women."

"It looks like I just did, miss smarty pants!" Borris was so proud of himself for that line. And I walked right into it.

"Good job. But I'm married. This is my wife, Brendolyn!" If she's going to smirk through this painful encounter, she's about to be a part of it.

Smiling way too big, she introduces herself. "Hi, I'm Dolly! It's actually Brendolyn like Lena just said, but no one calls me that except Jelena. Anyways, don't worry, we're not ACTUALLY married. We're just best friends who chose to be committed life partners! She's free as a bird!"

Jag-off! What good is having a wife if she doesn't let me use the 'married and taken' line when I don't want some fuckboy to think he can win me over?

"Oh! So do you ladies, like, do stuff?" he's intrigued.

"Fuck no! And especially not with you!" I rebuked. Disappointment covered his face. Damnit. Now I'm being the asshole.

"Look, Borris, where are your friends?" Borris shrugged. Fuck. He's a loser trying to be cool. I know Brendolyn is going to feel bad. The girl can't stand to know someone is left out astray.

"Well, why don't you hang out with us? We could always use a male for protection." There it is. She offered before I even finished my own thought. "But, just so you know, I will cut the fuck out of you if you think you're going to try and take advantage of our kindness!" There she is. My reverse sour-patch kid. First she's sweet, then she's sour, so everyone knows not to fuck with her.

"Oh, no worries. I won't. Thanks!"

Borris better be a chill dude, now that it looks like we're stuck with him for a week. I rolled my eyes and looked towards Melissa, who was just taking in the exchange without getting involved. She's a smart woman.

CHAPTER 3

Chapter Song:

"Kumbaya My Lord"

After way too long standing in the blistering hot sun, we finally made it through security and into the venue. We walked over to the camping grounds and looked for a good spot to set up camp. We collectively agreed on a spot about midway back, and off to the side, close to the tree line. That way we have some hope for shade if we need it. Then it was time to set up camp.

Melissa worked on the tent most of the time with Borris. She is a saint for asking him for help. The guy is already driving me nuts with his googly eyes on me all the time. Meanwhile, Brendolyn and I worked on the fire pit. There was already a ring of soot leftover from campfires-past, so we started there. Brendolyn decided she was 'Wendy" from Peter Pan when I asked her to go get firewood, and quoted, "Squa no fetchem firewood. Squa go home!" Then she laughed and went off to go fetchem the firewood.

After about an hour or so, our camp was set up. We didn't start the fire, though, because it was too hot for that shit. Brendolyn also packed solar powered twinkle lights she strung up around our campsite to bring in light, mark out our territory, and it gave it a nice hippy aesthetic to it. I didn't think it was quite necessary, but it does look nice, and it made emo sparklepants happy, so I let her do it.

The good bands weren't scheduled to hit the stages until later in the night, so we had time to kill before the real fun began. While we waited, we all split ways and walked around the venue. We scoped out the stages, found where the food stands were, priced everything, found the merch tables, and miscellaneous vendors, and really got a way of the land so we could come up with game plans in the days to come. Brendolyn made sure she got a corndog right away. Melissa and I split a giant fresh squeezed lemonade, and I don't know what Boring Borris was doing. I think he bought one of those surfer boy sea shell necklaces they sell at Hollister.

After a while I was pretty beat, and we still had the opening night to go, so I went back to the campsite to take a pretty hardy power nap. It must've been a good idea, too, because when I woke up, I found everyone else had decided to join me. Cuddle puddle.

It was pretty comfy, but I checked the time and it was getting late. Reluctantly, I got up and started preparing the campfire for dinner. We were going to need to eat something more than a corndog and lemonade if we wanted to make it through the night. So, I decided to cook up some beef cubes with peppers and onions in a cast iron skillet. I added some teriyaki sauce, and boiled up some water for rice. The smell of the food woke up Brendolyn. She groggily made her way over, looked at the meal and asked, "is it ready yet?"

I said, "Yeah, just about."

"Great! I'll wake up Melissa and Borris then!" Next thing I knew, she pulled a big old triangle out of a duffle bag and started clanking it and yelling "come 'n get it!" *Where the hell does this girl come from?*

An annoyed Melissa and Borris stumbled out of the tent. "Really Dolly? That wasn't necessary," Melissa grumbled as she glared at the country farm dinner bell in Brendolyn's hands. Brendolyn just grinned and said, "Sorry. I wanted to try it."

We all made plates and sat around the campfire to eat before we got cleaned up for the night. Of course Borris had to bring an acoustic guitar with him, and Brendolyn, who has zero vocal ability, decided it was a great opportunity to grace us with her version of an opening act. She sang all the hokey campfire songs. This girl hasn't even started drinking yet. But, as always, she was enjoying herself. I figured, if you can't beat 'em, join 'em, so I chimed in and sang the damn pine cone song with her. And Melissa joined in too. After a few songs, and getting past the obvious glares from people at neighboring campsites, it was all a fun and dandy time. I guess Borris is good for one thing. He can play a basic 3 chord song.

"Okay, so the first band starts at 8. It's 7:15 now. We should probably start getting ready," Melissa reminded us of the reason we were all here. Brendolyn jumped up and started throwing clothes all over the inside of the tent looking for whatever she packed for the first night.

"I just need to wash up and I'll be ready, so I'll clean up here, while you all do what you gotta do first," I offered. Everyone accepted my offer and headed to the tent to change, put on makeup, fix their hair, etc.; or so I thought.

"Hey pretty lady! Want some help?" The voice startled me.

"Holy Fuck! Borris, watch who you sneak up on. I almost cracked your skull with a hot skillet!"

"Sorry! I didn't mean to sneak up on you. I just didn't want to be in the tent while the ladies were changing. So I thought I'd offer you a hand." Well, that was considerate of him at least he's not trying to be a creep on my friends.

"Well, fine, you can help me put the food back into the cooler and lock it up so bears and drunks don't get into it," I suggested once I was able to catch my breath again and reason, "and moving forward, don't call me pretty lady. My name is Jelena."

"You got it Jelena!" He saluted.

"You don't need to stand at attention and salute me either, you weirdo. Just be chill."

"Chill. Got it. Don't worry. I'm cool as a cucumber!"

Gosh Borris is strange, or just really nervous. I can't tell which. I laughed and accepted his quirks. Melissa emerged out of the tent first. Brendolyn will take days to get ready.

"Alright, I'm up! Melissa, can you entertain Borris. I'm going to grab a quick shower and change."

"No problem. Borris, don't you need to change too?" Melissa asked.

"Yeah, but I'm waiting for my turn in the tent," he replied.

Melissa nodded. "Dolly, if you're dressed, come do your makeup out here so Borris can change his clothes," I yelled into the tent before I headed to the shower room.

When I got back, everyone was changed and ready for the festival, with beers and White Claw Surges in hand. "Want a drink?" Borris offered.

"No thanks. Alcohol gives me a headache. I'm fine with a water please." Borris reached into the cooler, handed me a water, and locked it back up for safe keeping.

"Alright homies, we ready to party?!" Brendolyn said.

"Yep. Let's go!" Said Melissa. And we were off.

CHAPTER 4

Chapter Song:

"Rock and Roll All Night" by Kiss

The set list is full of bangers and the first night is always a big medley of all the biggest artists being featured at the festival. We're talking the classics, the legends, and the newest big artists all on the same stage for the first night. It's like the Super Bowl halftime show extended to 4 hours and full of every emo, punk, metal head's wettest dreams. It's sick!

The show kicked off with Kiss playing 'Rock and Roll All Night'.

Those guys are in their 70s and still know how to put on one hell of a show. Other legends include Ozzy Osborne, Jon Bon Jovi, AC/DC, Scorpions, Journey, and Pat Benatar; just to name a few. For one week we have the evolution of rock from the 70s to the 2020s. Five decades of music, all in one place. Plus the show has pop-up small stages around for new up-and-coming artists, indie rock bands, and regular people attending the festival to get up and try their hand at the drums. There are scouts walking around in plain clothes, too, just looking for new talent. If you're lucky, someone like David Grohl just might invest in getting you signed under his label. This show is unlike any other before it. And I'm here. Taking it all in. Listening to all the best rock music that made history. This is about to be an experience of a lifetime.

ALthough, I have to admit, I'm not a fan of uberly crowded places. So I took some anti-anxiety meds, and my vertigo meds before we came out into the crowd. The main stage is beyond packed. Shoulder-to-shoulder is an understatement. And unfortunately, if someone wanted to target a mass shooting, this would be the place to do it. We're all packed like sardines. I really should have invested in bullet proof vests for this thing, now that I'm thinking about it. There've been so many mass shootings in the U.S. in recent years, we're all gonners for sure. Well, at least I'll be going out listening to the sweet sweet sounds of 'Highway to Hell' or maybe if I'm lucky it'll be 'Stairway to Heaven'. Time will tell.

The night went on like one would expect an epic night of its nature would; loud booming music, the vibrations pounding in my chest. I made sure to bring extra water, snacks, band-aids, etc. in my travel bag that is safely secured to my front right hip. I don't trust people not to try and mug me. It was too loud for conversations, which was great because then I didn't have to listen to whatever it was Borris was trying to mansplain to me all night. I have to give the guy some credit, he is trying. Why he's trying so damn hard is beyond me, but 'A' for effort. Melissa is pretty tall so she stood behind the group most of the time, just vibin'. Brendolyn bounced around dancing, singing, clapping, cheering, really being a part of the crowd. I like to mostly chill and take it all in. Really feel the music and watch the hard work the artists put in to entertain us. We're a drug free, drama free bunch, which I say works perfect for us. Borris, well, I just acquired him this morning, so I don't actually know what his deal is yet. But so far he seems okay enough.

As the night went on, I found myself growing more and more appreciative of the long nap. There's no way I'd have still been awake otherwise. All of the bands had been superb; young and old. There were some great collaborations too. They experimented with never before seen mash-ups and it seemed like the bands were having just as much of a good time as everyone else in the crowd. That's nice to see. I hate when I go to see a band and it looks like they don't even want to be there. I mean, I get it. Loud crowds, life on the road trapped in a tour bus with the same five people for a year, no breaks, playing the same set list on repeat night after night; it has to get mundane as hell. But that's what they signed up for. That's what touring is all about; it's bringing the music fans love to a live stage. It's feeling the energy of the crowd and using that as fuel to put on one hell of a show night after night. I'm not saying it's easy by any means. A lot of the music is complicated to perform in its own right, but it's also what they're paid the big bucks for. I'm not talking about measly artists who are struggling to pay for gas, I'm talking about the mega stars like Led Zeppelin or Blink 182. The ones who have paid their dues and built a big name and following for themselves. The real head-bangers.

I enjoyed the first night of the festival for as long as I could stay up for it. After several hours of festivities, the crowd started to get real rowdy; howling and carrying on like animals. It was probably close to 3 a.m. when I decided to call it a night.

"I'm beat. I'm heading back to the tent," I said to the group over the roar of the crowd.

"But you're going to miss the final act of the night," Brendolyn protested.

"That's ok. We have all week. Just take some videos of the good stuff," I said.

"Ok, well be careful heading back. Do you have a flashlight?"

"Yeah. I'm good."

"Maybe someone should walk with you just in case," Melissa suggested.

"I'll do it," Borris chimed in. Yeah, he's still here.

"I'm fine. I know my way," I said.

"I'd feel more comfortable if someone went with you," said Melissa.

"Yeah, I don't trust these people. Maybe you should let Borris walk with you. He's at least male. And Melissa and I will stay together, so we should be safe too. Buddy system!" Brendolyn suggested.

"Why do I end up with Borris in the buddy system?" I asked.

"Because it's your lucky day!" Borris chimed in. I rolled my eyes. "Look, I'm just going to make sure you get back safe. Besides, I'm getting pretty tired too."

"Okay, fine. Borris, you're coming with me," I reluctantly agreed. Borris was overjoyed. "But no funny business, you hear?"

"Oh no ma'am! I'm not one of those kinds of guys. I'll keep my hands to myself. That is, until you can't resist me anymore, and beg for my caress in the middle of the night. Then I'll have to oblige."

"Don't get your hopes up pal."

We walked back to the camp making small talk, much to my dismay. I would have been happy just walking back in comfortable silence, but Borris doesn't know how to be quiet. So I got to hear all about his toe nail fungus, and how the sweat in his socks is giving him trench foot; or so he thinks.

After we took turns changing into our nightwear, the two of us nestled up into our prospective sleeping bags and said our 'good nights'. It's been a long day, and I suspect it’s about to be an even longer week.

CHAPTER 5

Chapter Song:

"Here Comes the Sun" by The Beatles

I woke up to the smell of sweat and the blinding glare of the sun. Someone was up and left the tent entrance open. Asshole. I didn't know what time it was, but I was not happy about the heat and bright sky. I got myself up and out of the sleeping bag. Tossed my disheveled self together, and stumbled my way out of the tent.

Sunscreen, bug spray, water. Those were the first three things I grabbed out of the bag of supplies. Everyone was gone. No one was in the tent. No one was by the fire pit. Still unsure of the time, or why no one bothered to wake me up or tell me where they were going, I decided now would be a better time than any to take advantage of the shower room.

I gathered my toiletries and headed for the showers. I got washed up, reapplied the sunscreen and bug spray, pulled my hair up, and did all the other typical things you do first thing in the morning. To my surprise, the shower room and bathrooms were also pretty empty. Usually it wouldn't matter what time of day it is, these things are hot, crowded, and nasty. *What am I missing?*

I shrugged it off, and went back to our campsite. I started preparing a fire for some breakfast. While the skillet was heating up, I pulled out a map and itinerary for the day. I looked up at the sky to determine the time of day. It seemed to be around noon. Damn, I never sleep in this late. No wonder everyone is gone. It's not even breakfast time, but it's lunch time. Oh well. It's breakfast for me.

I finished making some eggs and putting it on some bread I toasted over the fire. I topped it with some cheese, and had myself a pretty good egg sandwich. I'll call it brunch. Then it was time to figure out where the hell everyone is.

No sooner was I thinking about getting up and looking for someone, an out of breath Borris came running up to camp.

"Great, you're up! Now quick, we need you!"

"What? Why? What's going on? Where's Melissa and Brendolyn at?"

"We're taking Dolly to the infirmary. Something's wrong," he said.

Oh Hell no! Not my wife!

"What's wrong?" I asked as I tossed a bucket of sand onto the fire and grabbed the bag of emergency supplies.

I let Borris lead the way. I wasn't sure if I should be scared, or nervous, or pissed. Is she hurt? Is she sick? Did she do something stupid? Borris wasn't talking. And that was concerning, considering broski usually never shuts up.

Thoughts swirled through my head of all the possible scenarios I'd be walking into. *I should have stayed up with the rest last night. I should have powered through, or took a longer nap yesterday. Why didn't I wake up this morning? Or why didn't I hear anyone coming to bed? Did they sleep? Did something happen after we came back to sleep? How did Borris find out then if that were the case? Did Melissa come back to get him? And again, no one bothered to wake me up and tell me what the fuck was going on?!*

"Are you alright?" I heard the sound of Borris' annoying voice break through my thoughts. "What?"

"You look dazed and confused. Are you okay? Or are you going to end up in the infirmary too?"

I snapped out of it. "Well, maybe I am dazed and confused. Why the Hell did no one bother to come get me until now?!"

"Woah! Chill. You were knocked out this morning. Then Dolly forgot shower shoes and walked back barefoot from the shower room. I think she stepped on something. She was bleeding and limping when she got back to the campsite. We didn't think, we just moved. Melissa and I helped carry her to the infirmary. But then she was complaining of a migraine, threw up, and passed out. That's when I came running back to get you," Borris finally explained in defense.

"Well is she okay?! Is she sick? Is it heat exhaustion? Dehydration? Did she have any water yet today? It's hot as balls out here, and she forgets to drink water," I jumped into mom mode.

"I don't know. That's why she's in the infirmary, and you're now here."

"Okay, let's go in and see what the nurse on staff has to say then." Borris is kind of good for nothing at this moment in time. But, at least he had the wits to come get me when he did.

We walked in and the place was packed. Well, I guess this is where everyone ended up. It's gotta be this heat. Borris guided me to where Melissa and Brendolyn were. Brendolyn was lying on a cot, barely conscious.

"Hey, do you need anything? I brought the emergency bag. Also, how's the foot? Borris said you were bleeding."

Brendolyn groaned. And somewhere in there she shook her head no, and kicked her bandaged and bloody foot up.

"The nurse gave her something for a migraine, and had her drink Pedialyte. She also wrapped up her foot. They want her to rest for a little bit before she'll be released," Melissa filled me in.

"Gotcha. Okay, well, I guess we'll just hang out here until she can go then."

And that's what we did. Fortunately someone was smart enough to pack a deck of cards in the emergency bag, so we started playing a few rounds of War. It was about two hours when Brendolyn woke up from her drugged stupor. Melissa and Borris were getting hungry. I don't think they had any breakfast, or lunch. We got the nurse to come over to check her out and see if we were all clear to leave. The nurse checked her vitals and looked her over, and gave us the go ahead.

Brendolyn was still pretty weak, so we helped her out. Borris went ahead of us and came back with some lemonade and a corndog. The man's learning. We went back to the campsite, and all decided to sit in the tent where there was shade. Brendolyn was able to lie down, and Melissa made sandwiches for everyone to eat. I still wasn't too hungry, so I snacked on some grapes we had in the cooler.

"Well, this day is just about shot," Melissa said.

"I'm sorry," grumbled a still sick Brendolyn.

"No reason to be sorry. It could have happened to any of us. We're just glad you're okay," Borris said.

"Yeah. Besides, I looked at the lineup for today and we didn't miss anything. It was mostly just some no name bands playing at the smaller stages. There's another big show tonight, but we can skip it if you're not feeling up to it," I reassured her.

"I think Asking Alexandria and May Day Parade are playing tonight. I'm not a hater, but they're not my favorite, so I'm fine with skipping one night," Melissa offered.

"Yeah, same here," I said.

"Yeah. I don't like them. But what about Borris?" Brendolyn asked.

"What? Nah. Don't worry about me. I'm just happy to be here. If it's something I really want to do, I'll just bounce and come back later. After all, I am party crashing your girls trip," Borris said. Well, at least he knows he's being a big party crasher.

"Okay. It's decided then. We're staying in tonight," I decided.

"Sounds good," Melissa agreed.

"Hey, was it just me and the drugs, but were they treating dogs or just very hairy people in that infirmary today?" Brendolyn sat up to question. A look of confusion and concern on her face.

Then I realized what she was talking about. I was so concerned about her, I didn't pay much attention to anyone else in the room being treated. But there was something eerie about how they looked.

I think we all had the same realization at the same time. Everyone exchanged the knowing glances around the tent.

"I'm going to make sure our supplies are locked up. And I'm bringing the food and emergency bag in the tent with us tonight," Borris said. Yep. We're staying in the closed-up tent tonight. It was decided without even needing to say it.

CHAPTER 6

Chapter Song:

"Who Needs Sleep?" by Barenaked Ladies

We didn't get much sleep that night. We couldn't sleep over the howls, and growls of what we're convinced were beasts in the night. Maybe setting up camp so close to the woods wasn't a smart idea after all.

We tried to distract ourselves from our crazed imaginations by listening to the roar of the crowd and the rock music echoing from the main stage. The show must go on; even if there's something so peculiar going on.

"Maybe we are all suffering from extreme heat exhaustion and are imagining things," I suggested.

"Maybe. Or we're just flat out exhausted," Melissa replied. She had been trying to get sleep for hours.

"But how does that explain the monstrous noises snarling from just outside our tent walls?" Brendolyn had a point.

"Well, whatever it is, let's just try not to think about it. Maybe we're just hearing someone's service dogs getting into a fight, or mating," Borris tried to reason. We all knew out of all the possibilities, that one wasn't it. But it was just as sane as any other thought we all had, so we accepted it and dropped the subject.

"Let's try and get some sleep. I'm sure everything will be fine by morning after we've rested," I said. I was pretty tired too. It had to be near 3 a.m.

"Good luck. I've been trying to fall asleep for 2 and half hours now." Melissa clearly isn't doing well on stress of the unfamiliar and little sleep. I don't blame her. We've had a crazy trip so far.

"You're right. Let's cuddle puddle and sleepy sleep," Brendolyn suggested. I wasn't a big fan of the cuddle puddle idea, but it might be our safest option for the time-being. I think we all had the same idea. So we pushed our sleeping bags and air mattresses closer together, and huddled up for the night.

I got no sleep. I'm pretty sure nobody got any sleep. Except for Borris who was heard snoring for a bit. He either slept through the night, or he managed all of 40 minutes of sleep. If that were the case, I'm sure it was no picnic for any of us.

The roar of the crowd and music died down about an hour after we decided to get some sleep. Then a drunken stampede stumbled its way through the campsite. If we were having trouble sleeping before, this certainly wasn't going to help. The parade of tired, drunk and high rock enthusiasts were far from a quiet bunch. I think locking up the food was protecting us more from strangers with the munchies, than it was from any curious grizzly bears. It sounded like they didn't know up from down, or whose tent was whose. If this is how it was the night before, I have no idea how I slept through it.

The after party on the campgrounds seemed to go until dawn. I wondered why these people never sleep. I was thankful that their chaos provided a good distraction from the supernatural sounds we were hearing earlier in the night. Maybe it really was just all in our heads afterall.

The sun began to rise. The birds started chirping, and finally there was a stillness in the air. Peace. Quiet. Nothing but the tranquil sounds of nature. I dozed off, and began to dream.

CHAPTER 7

Chapter Song:

"Sleepwalking" by All Time Low

I find myself standing in the middle of the music festival venue by the main stage. It's empty. Nobody in sight. Quiet. Silent. *Did I sleep through the shows? Did they shut the festival down? Did everyone die?* I don't know what's going on, but it's strange.

I walk away from the main stage and began to wander. Perhaps I'll find people somewhere else. Another small stage maybe. My feet are hurting as I walk. I look down to realize I have no shoes on. My feet are muddy and a little bloody from walking around without shoes. I figure there's nothing I can do about it now, so I decide to keep walking. I passed a food stand. The line is normally really long at this one. It serves cheesesteaks. But it's deserted. It's not closed and locked up, but instead it's as if it had been sitting vacant and abandoned for decades. But it was just operating yesterday. Weird.

I look around; still nobody is in sight. I decide to climb up on the counter and into the cheesesteak food truck. I look in the fryers; gross. It's full of old dried up grease, with a layer of dirt and debris caked on top. The peppers and onions are rotten; black and covered in bugs. The cooler is warm. The buns are stale. I'm glad I didn't eat from this place. The ipad to pay is offline; dead. Still no trace of anyone having been here in weeks, or months. *How long did I sleep for?*

Repulsed by the sights and smells of the dirt, mold, and grime in the food truck, I decide to leave and keep looking for some form of life. I make my way over to the parking lot area to see if the car is even still here. I don't know where Brendolyn or Melissa are. Quite frankly, I could care less where Borris ended up. Glad he's out of my hair.

As I cross the big field, I look around, keeping my eyes peeled for anyone, anything. Nothing. The more I look, the more uneasy I feel. The ground is coated in a thin layer of dark brown and black fur, like a pack of dogs shed all over the place. There's deep scratches and gashes in the structures I pass; tents, trash cans, porta potties, food trucks, etc. Everything is torn and beat up. *Maybe a tornado came through.*

I find a cluster of shoes on the ground. All different styles, and sizes. I pick one up to examine it closer. It's all tore up, like someone's feet were far too big; busting at the seams. Holes are worn in the sides of them. I put the shoe down and pick up a few others; all different shoes, all the same thing. Well, looks like there's no use in putting these on. *Maybe that's what happened to my shoes.*

I proceed to the parking lot to find the car. The closer I get, the more uneasy I begin to feel. Panic is welling up in my chest. My heart is pounding. It feels like it's going to burst out of my body. Terror. Pure terror. *But why? Why do I feel this way? What is on the other side of that hill where the cars are parked?* I fight my fears and keep going.

I make my way to the top of the hill, but just as I climb high enough to where I should be able to see the parking lot, I'm stopped, like I hit a wall. It feels like an electromagnetic field keeping me in. I can't break through. *Am I trapped? What's on the other side?*

More panic comes over me. I try to clear my head and get a grip of myself. I try again. No success. *Okay, maybe it's just this section. Let's just walk along this hill and see if I'm able to break through this barrier anywhere.*

I walk around the premise of the venue, trying to find a release of the pressure keeping me in. After what seemed to be about an hour of that with no luck, I find myself back where I started. The whole time, I saw not a single person.

Just as I sit down in the muddy, furry, sort of grassy hillside to take a break, I hear music. It's faint, and echoing off the sky? *Am I in some kind of biodome? Or bubble?* That's the only explanation for the force field I'm stuck in. The music sounds like a carousel; cymbals, horns, an accordion. *Is this some kind of sick carnival?*

I get up to follow the sound. Maybe that will lead me to a person, or at least bring me some answers instead of all this wandering around with anxiety. I walk down the hill and head over in the direction of the practice stages. There's sound systems back there that would be able to project the music I'm hearing. I get half way there and the music changes.

"Terror Time" by Skycycle

The immediate sense of childhood nostalgia that the song brought me was quickly followed with fear. Remembering the scene in the 'Scooby-Doo on Zombie Island' movie the song is featured in, I was all too familiar with what's likely about to happen next. I look around the empty bowl of the venue, expecting to see something, or someone. Nothing. *Maybe this is all just in my head.*

I turn back around to head in the direction I was walking in, and find myself face-to-face with a hairy, snarling beast. Startled, and instantly terrified, I let out a yelp, and about-face and fucking bolt it! Fight or flight. Turns out I am not a fighter. I hear the music getting louder and I run harder. I head for the food trucks. The monster is on my heels. Somehow with the help of my adrenaline rush, I'm able to leap over the counter and into the food truck. I frantically stumble to figure out how to close the window. I find a rope and I pull it. The window slams closed just as the monster lunges to get in. The animal's bear-sized paw gets caught in the window. I hear it yelp, and hurry to lift the door just enough to free its paw. I didn't want to hurt the bloodthirsty creature. I just wanted to get away from it. No sooner did it pull its paw away, I quickly slam the door shut again and latch it.

Then run to the side door and make sure it's locked up tight too. I can hear the beast from outside the food truck growling, howling, and circling the truck. It might be strong enough to knock this thing over, but it's the best form of shelter and protection I got right now.

A few moments go by and it gets quiet again. I don't have the nerve to open the door to peer out to see if the coast is clear. Instead, I'm just going to hunker down here and see if there is anything salvageable to eat. Turns out I'm in a taco truck. Everything is pretty rotten. But the tortilla shells seem okay. I snack on the stale crunchy ones. Then I remember I'm hiding out, so I shouldn't be so noisy. I switch my snack to the soft floury tortillas. It's bland, but at least it's something.

"Hero" by Weezer

It's now that I realize the music playing is quieter again. 'Terror Time' is over. A new song is playing now. I stop chewing and sit still to listen; trying to identify the new song. It's 'Hero' by Weezer. It's a good song. *I wonder if this means the monsters are gone.*

I sit and listen to the song. Finally able to catch my breath a little bit. Weezer was one of the groups that was supposed to be performing this week. *We see how well that turned out. Unless, maybe it's a live song. They might be on the practice stage.*

I stuff the rest of the tortillas in my pocket, and get up to go investigate if the coast is clear. I peek out a little window in the door. I don't see any signs of life. I decide to go for it. I gently unlock the door, and slip out of the food truck. It's a wide open field, so there's no protection in case there is anything out there. I turn around and go back in the food truck. I look for something I can use for protection. I find an umbrella, and a big metal serving spoon. *Okay, I'm armed. Time to investigate, and find my way out of this place.*

I begin my stroll out of the food truck and across the field towards the practice stage. I keep the sounds of the song in focus, trying not to let fear or anxiety get to me. I'm nearly to the practice stage, when the song ends. Silence. I begin to feel uneasy again. I pick up the pace to get there quicker. I turn the corner to go behind the main stage where the practice stage is located. That was a big mistake.

I'm faced with hundreds of wolves. Giant ones. Some sleeping. *Shit it was a trap. The whole pack is here. Fuck, I walked right into their den.* I run. It's now that I realize my spoon and umbrella aren't going to protect me for shit. I'm out numbered. I can't outrun them. They're hungry and angry, and I'm their prey.

I slip in the mud, twist my ankle and down I go. *I'm a gonner.* I feel the weight of the beasts pounce onto my body; crushing me.

CHAPTER 8

Chapter Song:

"Chop Suey!" by System of a Down

I was startled awake, and crushed between a hard wooden floor and a heavy load on top of me.

"Wake-Up!" I heard Borris yell/whisper at me. That must be who tackled me in my sleep.

"What the fuck Borris?!" I groaned at him. I was displeased. Although I was a bit relieved that nightmare was over. That's when I remembered the dream.

"Sorry! Sorry! You were freaking out in your dream. I had to stop you," he explained. I was still a bit shaken up from the dream.

"Are you okay?" He asked, "what were you dreaming about?" A look of deep concern was in his eyes. I didn't know what it was like for him, but it was certainly Hell for me.

I looked around and realized we weren't in the tent. It was dark out, and we were on an old beat up stage. It must've been one of the original stages that they didn't use anymore. This venue dates back to the 70s.

I sat up and looked around, still a little shaken up. The anxiety certainly didn't leave with the dream. I looked at Borris and prepared myself to retell the nightmare.

"I was trapped in the venue. I couldn't get out. And I was all alone. Everyone was gone. The food was rotten, the stages were destroyed. Then there was creepy circus music playing and it kept changing in the dream like a sound track. As I tried to find civilization or a way out, I ended up getting chased by a fucking monster wolf! I hid out in a nasty taco truck, and when I thought the coast was clear I snuck out and went towards the back of the main stage. That's when I found the entire pack of wolves. There were hundreds of them, drooling and growling. I tried to run, but I was dinner. You tackled me just as they started to maul me."

Borris stared in shock, jaw-dropped. "Fuck! That's terrifying. I'm so sorry. Glad I was able to rescue you awake though!" He grinned. I lightly punched him in the shoulder, "Thanks. It would have been nice if you woke me up a little gentler."

"You were freaking out and running. I didn't know what else to do," he said.

"Yeah, how did we get all the way out here to begin with?"

Borris prepared himself to tell his Experience.

"You were wrestling in your sleep in the tent. Tossing and turning. That’s what initially woke me up. I was lying there trying to go back to sleep to no luck. I could tell you weren't having a very good dream for how much you were tossing back and forth. I actually thought about gently waking you up then, but I was tired and warm and didn't want to move. It wasn't getting any better though, so I decided I should wake you. No sooner did I sit up, did you spring up and book it out of the tent. It kind of scared me. I didn't know what was happening. I thought maybe you woke up and had to pee or something. But something didn't feel right, and I didn't know what dangers were outside, so I grabbed a flashlight for protection and followed you. You ran all the way to this old stage and tripped. I wasn't expecting it and I tripped trying to stop. That's when I fell on you. I wasn't planning on tackling you awake that hard. But you were freaking the fuck out, and I'm clumsy."

"Sorry about that. I didn't intend to cause such a disturbance," I said.

Borris brushed it off, "Nah, don't worry about it. I'm just glad you're okay."

I caught myself blushing. *Dammit Borris! You're not supposed to be sweet and caring! I don't want to like you!* I quickly wiped the smirk right off my face, hoping it was too dark for Borris to notice. It wasn't though, and he was too pleased with himself, he just had to call me out.

"Do those pretty pink cheeks mean you might actually like me?" He smirked.

"No! I just appreciate you for looking out for my safety, you douche." *Smooth, Lena, smooth.* He didn't buy it. He just smiled and nodded in agreement.

"So what the hell time or day is it anyway? " I asked.

"I think it's around 8 ish of day three. You slept the day away dear."

"Don't call me dear. And fuck! I missed All Time Low?! Where is everyone?"

"Yeah. I'm sorry. We tried to wake you, but you were out. The show was kinda lame anyway. Most of the festival goers were up all night too and slept the day away. I don't know what it is. Maybe the uber late night on day one is what fucked up everyone's sleep schedule."

"Yeah, or they're all werewolves," I muttered. I still wasn't convinced that my dream wasn't foreshadowing reality.

Borris gulped in fear, "Do you really think that's what it is?"

"I mean, all the signs are kind of there. If you believe in that shit, which I don't think I do, but it does make sense. The howling, the hairy people in the infirmary," I reasoned.

"Fuck. Well, what do we do? I just thought maybe there were coyotes out last night." That was a lie. We both knew it. He was just trying not to sound so crazy probably.

"Well if my dream had anything to do with it, there are werewolves at this music festival. And I bet if we go back stage of the main stage, we'll find proof."

"Do you want to go check it out?" Borris asked.

"Fuck no! I just died in my dream for doing just that! I am not risking that shit in real life."

"Good point. Okay, so what do we do?"

I shrugged. I didn't know what to do.

"Well, are you hungry? We can grab something to eat."

"Not from a food truck. I'm still queasy from the dream. Let's head back to camp and eat something."

"Maybe not right now. I think one of the ladies is tent-ertaining."

"Oh. Got it. Ok, well I guess we'll just hang out here for a bit more until batwoman signals it's safe to return," I said, testing him to see if he catches the flaws in that statement.

"Um, I hate to break it to you, but that's not how the bat signal is used," He corrected me. Alright, he passed.

"I know. It was a good analogy though, so just go with it." He went along with it.

Borris and I sat and chatted a while longer. Basic small talk. He filled me in on everything I missed throughout the day. I was still bummed I missed All Time Low. They're one of my favorites. I've seen them before, though, so I guess it's okay. Plus, I think they'll be back out for a final performance on the last day, so I'll be able to catch the highlights of the show.

CHAPTER 9

Chapter Song:

"The Rock Show" by Blink 182

"So which group are you looking forward to seeing most?" I asked.

"Blink 182 for sure!" Borris responds.

"Solid choice. Good old 90s classic. I like it."

"Yeah! You know, I've always wanted to be in a band like that. When I was a kid, I used to practice all my favorite Blink songs to perform them. I never had the nerve to do it in front of anyone though," Borris confessed.

"Well it's not for everyone," I said. Then a light sparked in his eyes; excitement. He sat up straighter and got closer to me. *Oh no, I know where this is going.*

"Let me perform for you."

"What? No. Borris, it's okay. You don't have to do that."

"No, I want to. I want to finally have the chance to do this. Please," He looked at me, pleading. *Fuck. Here we go.*

"Fine. I'll be your audience. Sing away Borris," I sighed in defeat. He grinned real big and jumped up on the broken stage.

"Okay, Jelena, this one's for you." He took a breath, licked his lips and prepared to sing. I was nervous to be honest. I wasn't sure what I was about to witness.

"*Yeah, this song is dedicated to every kid who ever got picked last in gym class.*"

"Good Charlotte?" I asked.

Borris looked a little embarrassed. "Uh, no. Dammit. Wrong song. Okay, let me try again." He paused, and took another breath, and started again.

"*You like D&D, Audrey Hepburn, Harry Houdini, And Croquet. You can't swim, you can't dance, and you don't know karate. Face it, You're never gonna make it. I don't wanna make it. I just wanna…*"

"Oh! My Chem! Good choice, Borris!" I interrupt his beginning dialogue to compliment him."

"Fuck! No. Dammit. Wrong song again."

"Oh. Well, what song are you trying to sing? Maybe I can help you remember how it starts," I suggested.

"No, no. I got it. I just need a minute to think. I'm nervous. I've never done this."

"Okay. I'll wait." I sat and waited for Borris to remember the song he so desperately wanted to sing. I was beginning to think he really was a moron after all. But, I tried giving him the benefit of the doubt. We've been listening to a medley of bands all week, with little sleep, and a possible werewolf outbreak to boot.

"Alright. I figured it out. I'm sure of it this time!" He recentered himself. Took another long breath, and began his song.

"*Hanging out behind the club on the weekends. Acting stupid, getting drunk with my best friends. I couldn't wait for the summer and the Warped Tour. I remember it's the first time that I saw her there…"*

"Now that's a Blink 182 song! Appropriate choice for our setting," I encouraged him, as he continued to sing on. It's a catchy song that I was very familiar with. It was a shower concert favorite on my Pandora Station.

"*Because I fell in love with the girl at the rock show. She said, "What?", and I told her that I didn't know,"* Borris continued on. I tried not to read into the song lyrics that were coming out of his mouth, and just enjoyed the melody instead.

He sang his heart out through the whole song. Once he got warmed up, he was pretty animated in it as well; a true rock star at heart.

"I'll never forget tonight with the girl at the rock show," Borris concluded.

I had to admit, it wasn't bad. In fact, I caught myself bopping along to it by the end. Of course I knew the song. And this time, he was actually singing a Blink 182 song, like he said. I still wasn't quite sure how he managed to get them confused with Good Charlotte or My Chemical Romance, but it is what it is. He wasn't half bad. I was surprised about that. He actually might be half as talented as some of the small stage acts that have been playing throughout the days here.

When he finished, he took a small bow, and I applauded. Not too aggressively, but a polite applause. I'm sure it wasn't easy. He grabbed his elbow and looked away bashfully.

"Well done. You even remembered all the lyrics," I complimented.

"Thanks. Did you like it?" He asked. *Ugh fishing for compliments.*

"Yeah, it was tight. It was no Blink, but it was pretty solid. I'll give you that," I wasn't going to lie to him. But I also wasn't going to over inflate his ego either. A good, humble bout of honest criticism goes a long way, in my opinion.

Borris, still a little out of breath from his punk performance, sat down next to me on a wooden bench I moved to when he took the stage to sing his song. I knew he put a lot of energy and courage into the song, but he had a funny look on his face; a look, I was skeptical to try to read into. I didn't particularly want to know what the look meant. So I did my best to give him space, look away, and try to ignore it.

Then he made his move. Mother fucker just swooped in and kissed me!

Naturally unprepared, and freaked out a bit, because my oblivious ass did NOT see that coming, backed away.

"Woah! What are you doing that for?!" I asked a bit aggressively.

I immediately felt bad because I could tell I embarrassed Borris. For as many rocks instead of brain cells he has, somewhere there were mixed signals, and I just made an asshole move. Woops.

"Oh, uh. Sorry. I guess, I just, I thought it was okay. I sang you that song. I, I was trying to kind of tell you how I feel. I'm, fuck. I'm sorry. I thought when you said I did a good job, you knew I meant it was about you…"

He continued circling the drain, stumbling over his words, trying to explain himself and apologize for his move. I realized how I totally missed what he was trying to do all along. I wasn't sure if I should have been offended, like did he really think I was that shallow for something like that to actually work on me? Or was this really the best he got? I realized regardless, he was pretty nerdy, and seemed super nervous, and I made it awkward. In an instant, I lost a few brain cells, and my barely existent spontaneity miss fired, and the next thing I knew, I lunged forward and shut the mother fucker up by pressing my mouth to his.

Dammit Lena. This is the best we got? What am I doing this for?! Do I even like Borris? He seems pretty into you, considering the song he chose to sing. What the fuck am I doing?!... Actually, this isn't half bad. He doesn't seem all that bad of a person. Maybe this might be something. What does this mean for the camping situation? I got news for him, this is as far as this is going to go!

My inner dialogue was going A-wall while Borris quickly recovered from the shock of my suddenly kissing him. His hands moved into my hair and one on my waist as our bodies melted in closer to each other. I hated myself for enjoying it so much, I still do a bit. But I couldn't deny the fact that it wasn't half bad. In fact, it was actually pretty amazing. Who would've thought old Borris would have so many hidden talents?

CHAPTER 10

Chapter Song:

"Werewolves of London" by Warren Zevon

Borris and I spent the remainder of the evening making out, only pausing long enough to come up for air. I was surprised at how much of a gentleman he was being. Usually horn dogs like he tries to portray himself to be on the surface, would have tried to slide into second or third base. But he kept it right where it started, which is just as far as I'm comfortable with.

Then my stomach started to growl. Mood killed.

Borris pulled away, flushed and out of breath, he smiled, "Let's get you something to eat." I wasn't going to argue. It had been hours since my last meal. He grabbed me by the hand and helped me up. It wasn't until now, that I realized how secluded of an area we were in. *How far did I run?!* The old beat-up stage was lost under the canopy of trees and camouflaged by overgrown vegetation. Borris guided me towards where the food trucks were, instantly triggering flashes of my dream. I calmed my instant anxiety and reminded myself that it was just a dream, and concert goers were all around enjoying the festival like normal.

We stopped in the middle to survey our options. The line for Teriyaki chicken kabobs was relatively short, so we opted for that with some rice. It was a bit pricey, but everything is jacked up at this place. After we got our food, we walked around looking for a bench or table or someplace to eat it. Eventually we found a spot.

"This place really fills up at night more than anything," I said casually. Completely ignoring what all just went on, and acting like Borris and I are just chill. I was hoping it would distract him and send a message that I didn't want to talk about it. I was really just waiting to process my thoughts when I had some time to myself.

"Yeah. I imagine it's likely because the big name artists play at night. So people party all night and sleep all day. You know, as true rock does."

"Fuck yeah! Party on! Sex, drugs, and rock 'n roll!" I joked. Borris laughed. I was glad he wasn't dense enough to take me so seriously. I could never tell with him.

"Alright, Chinese food!" A stranger sat down on the bench next to us and just started up a conversation. We looked over to him and he was smiling at our plates of kabobs and rice. He tapped his plate of lo mein to mine as he said "Cheers mate!"

"Sup," I said with a nod. "Do you know him?" Borris whispered. "Nope," I said.

"Name's Willy." The stranger said as he stuffed his chopsticks into his noodles and offered his hand for an introductory shake. Being the polite person that I am, I took it and replied, "Lena." He was surprisingly hairy.

"Borris."

"Right. So what group are you here for?" Willy asked. Borris and I looked at each other and shrugged, "Everyone really. I like music," I said.

"Yeah, I'm just here for Blink 182, and meeting pretty ladies like this gal!" Borris said with a douchey smile as he wrapped his arm around my shoulder, scooting me closer to him and further from Willy.

"Nice! I'm here for Warren Zevon and Iron Maiden. Came all the way over from London," Willy seemed pretty proud of himself. As if airplanes can only fly from Europe.

"That's sick bro! My sister and I went backpacking through Europe once about five years ago. I like how you named your toilets Lou," Borris was great at small talk, or something like that. He could find something in common with an old oxidized penny.

"Ah yes. Americans don't call them lavertories either."

"No. We don't, Willy." I was over this dude already. "Where are you friends?" "Oh, I came alone." *Of course he did.*

"Right on! Me too!" Borris chimed in.

"Great, then why don't you two be friends, and I'm going to go find the ones I actually came here with?" I said, clearly annoyed at how these men think they can just intrude in my life without my asking them to.

"It was nice meeting you Willy. Enjoy your time here before returning back to London," I said as I got up and walked away. I really didn't care all that much that he sat down and was making conversation unprovoked, I was just getting a growingly uneasy feeling in my stomach the longer I sat there in the testosterone sandwich. Plus I was thirsty, so I headed in the direction of the fresh squeezed lemonade.

As I was standing in line, I looked over in the direction of the bench I came from. Willy and Borris were still there talking. Borris looked uncomfortable too, but he could just as easily get up and walk away like I did if he really wanted to. Neither of them looked very chipper anymore. Their conversation appeared to have taken a more serious turn, which isn't much of Borris's character from what I've gathered so far. I wondered what they were talking about, but then it was my turn to order, so I turned my focus back on the task at hand; thirst quenching lemon shake.

CHAPTER 11

Chapter Song:

"Somebody's Watching Me" by Rockwell

"Hey, where've you been? We were sleeping and when I woke up, you and Borris were gone," Melissa said, scaring the shit out of me.

"Whoa! Where'd you come from?"

"I was in line behind you at the lemonade stand," she replied. Her story checked out, she had a lemon shake in her hand. I nodded, "Yeah, I don't know, apparently I had a shit dream and ended up sleepwalking. Borris said I woke him up and he followed me. But that feels like hours ago. I've been eating and wandering around this place since," I said. I didn't want to get into all the details of how the night had actually been going.

"Well I'm glad you're safe, and that Borris made sure of it. Dolly and I were worried sick. We were looking everywhere."

"I thought Brendolyn had someone over in the tent," I said.

Melissa looked confused. "What? Not that I know of. We've been searching for you ever since we woke up and saw you were missing. What made you think that?"

"Borris said she was," I replied.

Melissa, being a logical matter-of-fact thinker was quick to respond, "Well, if we were all asleep and Borris followed you out of the tent when you started to sleepwalk, then how would he know if we had guests in the tent or not to begin with?" She had a valid point.

"I don't know. I didn't think about it. Maybe you guys snuck someone in during the day while I was still sleeping," I offered, trying to give Borris the benefit of the doubt. Although, he was starting to look pretty sketchy to me.

"No. We all had a shit night and didn't get much sleep. We caught a couple small bands, but didn't have the energy in the hot sun to make new friends or any of that. I wonder what gave Borris that idea," Melissa said.

I shrugged. "Who knows. Maybe he dreamt it. He's an odd one." Melissa agreed, and we dropped the subject.

"So where is Brendolyn anyway?" I asked after a few moments passed.

"I don't know. We split up to cover more ground looking for you a while ago. I’m sure she’ll turn up when she gets hungry.” Melissa made a good point. Brendolyn never missed a meal. She loved food far too much to let that ever happen.

CHAPTER 12

Chapter Song:

"Cut Deep" by Matt Maeson

"Speak of the devil. She must be hungry. Here she comes now!" I said as I saw Brendolyn running up towards us. It looked like she was limping a bit, but she always looks like a wounded duck when she runs, so it's hard to tell. It could just be the cut on her foot from yesterday too.

"Is she okay?" Melissa asked with concern in her voice. That told me, this wasn't her usual awkward looking run. "That cut on her foot looked like it was getting infected earlier," she mentioned.

Before I had the chance to respond, the wounded looking woman plowed right into me like a linebacker. "We have to go!" She stammered out of breath.

"Why? What's wrong?" I asked, holding her limp body up as she leaned most of her weight on me.

"Werewolves! I'll explain later. Just run to the woods! Melissa, get the first aid kit please."

"On it! I'll meet you there," Melissa ran off. *How much did I miss while I was sleeping?!*

We staggered off into the woods near our camp. When we finally reached a spot with a fallen tree we could sit on and rest, I insisted Brendolyn fill me in on what the Hell happened.

"We should wait for Melissa too."

"No. We can catch Melissa up later whenever she gets here," I said.

"Okay. Well, here's what happened. Yesterday I hurt my foot. I cut it on glass or a stick or something and then got sick and ended up in the infirmary."

"Yes, I know that much. Fast forward," I said.

"Okay, I'm just recapping. So we all tried to sleep and crazy shit was happening all night and into the morning. I dozed off a bit around noon I think, but then when I woke up, you and Borris were gone. Melissa and I went looking for you, but my foot was still hurting a bit from the day before. Melissa was concerned it was getting infected, so I changed the bandage and popped some antibiotics the nurse gave me and moved on with my life.

Anyway, we couldn't find you in this giant place, so we eventually decided to split up to cover more ground. I made my way over to some of the smaller stages and despite all the dry heat we've had, it was a total mud hole because someone knocked over one of the water barrels. So My feet got all wet and muddy, and my cut started hurting pretty bad. I found a rain barrel that wasn't knocked over and decided to use it to clean off my foot. It fucking burned like a bitch! But who knows what kind of bacteria is living in the stagnant rain water we're all expected to drink," she cringed. Brendolyn was always a bit of a germophobe.

"Go on," I pressed her to continue.

"Right, so nasty water. Cleaned the wound. And I moved on to look near the main stage because there was hardly anyone over by the small stage I was at. The music was bumpin! I'm pretty sure we were missing Bowling for Soup. So I got distracted and stopped and watched the band for a bit. I mean, that is the whole reason why we came here in the first place, and I love Bowling for Soup. I thought there was a good chance you and Borris were just here listening to the band too, and it was all fine.

But anyways, I was really feeling the music. The vibrations, pounding in my chest, reminding me why I love live music so much. Then I started to feel really sick again. I wondered if I had accidentally drank that water, because my stomach just instantly turned. I felt like my insides were going to turn out. I remember looking around to find the nearest garbage can, and that's when I noticed everyone seemed to be looking a bit how I felt. I don't know if everyone drank the water or what, but people were *not* okay!

I noticed the hair on my arms stood up. It looked longer and darker and thicker than I remember it being, but it could have been my imagination. I didn't get a good look at it because it was dark. That, and no sooner did I notice it, I was on the ground being dragged by some man in a black hat like Slash. Only it wasn't Slash. His hair wasn't curly. And the man was super hairy. I thought he must be Italian. And of course all of this is going through my head while I'm being dragged and pretty sure I was about to be kidnapped and sold into sex trafficking or something. I tried to squirm, but his massive hand had a really tight grip on my wrist. I considered chewing my hand off, but that was going to be too difficult. He dragged me through the crowd and all the way back stage of the main stage. He had brown/red eyes like they were pulsing with blood. And a snarl like a beast. It was terrifying. I thought for sure I was about to be food or raped or I don't know what. His breath smelled like stale liquor and lo mein. It was dark, so it was hard to tell, but it looked like he was turning into a wolf or something, like in 'Thriller'. I was holding my breath trying not to draw too much attention.

I thought maybe this was like 'Twilight' and he could smell my blood or something. I don't know. Something startled him, and the next thing I knew, I was stuffed in a big box the roadies pull gear out of. It was dark and crammed, but I felt a little safer at this point. Although, that's when my side started to hurt. I think I bruised a rib or something. I heard a howl, and grumbling. An angry, but familiar voice. I felt myself fading in and out of consciousness, and it was hard to focus on what was happening. It sounded like someone with a deep, menacing British accent. There was a clear scuffle happening. I wasn't sure why. I think I heard someone say something like, 'You fucking beast murdered my sister! I will not let you kill my friend too!'"

Brendolyn paused. I could tell she was processing this for the first time as she told it. It was all playing back in her eyes. The pieces were coming together. I put my hand on her leg to comfort her, although I'm shit at doing that. She knows it though.

Brendolyn snapped out of her dazed look and continued, "Then there was a yelp. Lot's of yelps and whimpering. I tried to climb out of the box to peek at what was going on. That's when I realized who the familiar voice was. It was Borris. He grabbed my hand and frantically pulled me out. He told me to run and hide in the woods and take you guys with me. That it wasn't safe here. I was scared and confused and in pain so I didn't argue or ask questions. I just wanted to get away from the wolf man who I'm pretty sure was about to eat me. I don't know what happened, but from the sounds of it, I think someone is dead. And I don't know if it was the monster or Borris. Or both. I just ran. And now my foot is fucking killing me. I think the wound is festering. I was so thirsty, it felt like I had rabies and was foaming at the mouth. So I dared to take a sip of the nasty water, and

I kept on running until I found you and Melissa."

Well shit. That was a lot to take in. My head was spinning with all the information. *Was Borris a killer? Is it true what Brendolyn heard? Are the painkillers getting to her?*

"What the fuck is it with these werewolves?!" Yep, that's the question I opted to go with.

"Yo, I don't fuckin know, but there's no way anyone can convince me they're not real. They are. We can't deny it. I saw him. And I don't know what's up with Borris either, but he saved my life."

"Damn. I was just with him, but some guy from London came up to us and started making small talk that annoyed me so I walked away. I was literally just talking to Melissa and drinking lemonade, and all of this was happening?! What the fuck?!.... And Holy Fuck! When did you get here?!" I exclaimed. I turned my head and saw Melissa just hovering in the fucking darkness holding a big ass bottle of peroxide.

She chuckled, "I've been standing here since Dolly said she was being kidnapped. I didn't want to interrupt her story. But I have peroxide for the wound. We should get that infection taken care of before you become a wolf lady next."

"You don't think I'm going to turn into one of them, do you?!"

"I don't know. We don't know if these people all came here like this, or if it's something here causing it to spread, like a virus, or a bite, or something." Melissa had a point. We didn't know what was causing this, but it did seem like the longer we stayed here, the more strange things were happening. And my dream sure didn't calm my nerves.

"Okay, let's get this over with. Foot," Melissa demanded of Brendolyn. She complied and unbandaged her foot and lifted it in Melissa's direction.

"It's festering," She said in disgust. Then she poured nearly the whole bottle of peroxide on it.

"Bloody Hell, Melissa, that hurts!"

"Did the British beast turn you?!" I asked.

Brendolyn chuckled, "No. I just thought maybe the pain wouldn't be so searing if I pretended to be Ron Weasley. It didn't work though."

"You're so strange," I told her. She smiled in confirmation and said, "I know!"

Melissa made sure to dry the wound and thoroughly bandage it up tight again. "That will have to hold. Hopefully it doesn't get any worse.

I'd hate to have to scrape the infection out with a knife."

"Yeah, no thanks. I'll just die of gangrene first." Melissa rolled her eyes. "You're not going to die of gangrene. We'll be long home from the music festival and back in civilization before that happens. The ribs, I got nothing for you. You're just going to have to take shallow breaths until it heals." Brendolyn let out a sigh of aggravation to that news.

Some time passed on. "So what are we waiting here for anyways? Do you think it's safe to head back to camp?" I asked.

"No, Borris said we had to hide out in the woods," Brendolyn insisted.

"Well, where is he anyway?" I asked.

"Right behind you," I heard Borris' voice say from behind me. I nearly jumped off the log I was sitting on.

"Holy fuck! You scared the shit out of me!" I yelled, and punched him.

"Ow! Sorry. Geeze Lena, be gentler. I'm sore," Borris groaned. That's when I got a better look at him. He was all beat up and covered in fur and blood. I didn't want to know if the blood was his or someone else's.

"What the hell happened to you?!"

CHAPTER 13

Chapter Song:

"Welcome to the Chaos" by Fame on Fire

"I killed him." Borris said. We all stared in silence; in disbelief.

"You killed who?" Melissa asked.

"Willy. The werewolf of London. I had to. He was going to kill Dolly, and he was going to kill me. Hell, he was going to kill everyone. And I'm not usually one for violence, but I couldn't let that happen. He's not human. He's a monstrous beast, and he had to die." Fear and pain seeped through the sound of his voice.

"Fuck," Brendolyn said, letting his words sink in.

"I mean, how do you know? Maybe he confused her for someone else. Maybe a girlfriend and that's just how he seduces her," I tried. I knew it sounded dumb as I was saying it, but so does 'the man was a werewolf', so my stupid explanation should get a pass. But I was desperately grasping at straws trying to find any kind of reason that didn't point to my dream foreshadowing how this week would end.

Borris looked at me dead-pan. "He wasn't trying to flirt. He was trying to feast." Ouch. His words were sharp and cutting. But he was probably right.

"So you stabbed him with a stake?" Brendolyn asked.

"No Buffy, that's how you kill vampires," He corrected her.

"Oh. Sorry I had the wrong mythical creature," she sassed. I punched her. "This is serious! You were almost FOOD you bitch!" I corrected her. I wasn't mad at her. That's just how you have to talk to her to get it through her hard head sometimes.

"Okay. I'm sorry. Thank you for doing whatever it is you do to kill a werewolf in my honor," she said.

"You're welcome," Borris proudly accepted the apology.

"So, wait. If they were backstage, how did you know she was in trouble?" Melissa asked. *Ah, a hole in his plot.*

"Well, after Lena left me over there on the bench with the barbarian, he pissed me off. We had words. Words of the past. He remembered me and I most certainly remembered him, but I wasn't going to bring it up in front of my lady."

"I'm not your lady," I interjected.

"Not now," he quickly responded. As if he knew that was coming before he even said the words. He continued his explanation to Melissa in the same breath. "So there's been some bad blood between us for some time. I hadn't seen him since the night something really terrible happened, and I've been traveling solo to music festivals ever since, trying to prevent the terrible thing from happening again."

"What's the terrible thing?" I asked.

"I'll get there. So to answer your question, I didn't trust him. Weird things were happening all week, and I suspected something like this was at play. After he walked away, I got lost in the crowd so I could keep an eye on him. Then I saw him eye up a girl. I didn't even realize who it was at the time. I just knew I couldn't let it happen again. So I kept a distance, but a steady pace and I followed him. Once I saw him grab you, I ran as fast as I could to try and stop him. I'm not a very good runner, and he was quick. I was terrified it'd be too late by the time I finally caught up. Fortunately it wasn't. But the blood was boiling in me. I wasn't planning on killing him. Just getting you away from him and safe. But then memories of the past flashed before me. All the pain, guilt, and regret, came over me, and I ended him once and for all.

Dolly, I didn't want you to see what happened next. I didn't know who was going to die or live, and I didn't want to scar you like I've been all these years."

"Okay, so what the hell happened all these years ago that triggered you so much?" Brendolyn asked.

Borris closed his eyes tight and took a deep breath. I could tell, this was something he really wasn't comfortable talking about. But we probably needed to know.

"He killed my sister."

CHAPTER 14

Chapter Song:

"Hunter's Moon" by Ghost

"WHAT?!" I exclaimed.

"Yeah, she and I were backpacking through Europe. We planned to spend the whole summer hopping from music festival to music festival and living life to the fullest for one summer. It was right after we graduated from college. We were twins. It was like our last hoorah before we got real jobs and went off to live our separate adult lives. We'd planned it for years.

About halfway through the summer, we were at a festival in a desolate town outside of London. All the raw stripped down indie artists were there. It was like life in the 60s. It was going just how we always dreamed it would. We camped, hitch-hiked, made friends, the whole bit. Willy was with a group we made friends with. They were a hairy lot, but it was Europe, so I didn't think anything of it. Well, I should have noticed the signs. They were wolves. Werewolves. And their pack traveled from music fest to music fest, feasting on their prey, and after each festival the pack got larger and larger. I don't know if they were turning them, or if it was the water, or werewolves just use these types of gigs to gather or what. I haven't figured that part out yet. But by the end of the festival, my sister's body was torn to shreds. He seduced her like he was some special lover, and then he ripped her heart out right before her eyes. I saw it happen. But I was too far away. I was in line to use a porta pot and by the time I realized he was attacking her, and I ran over to intervene, it was too late. She was dead. He and his pack fled. I've been going to music festivals solo ever since. To continue to live out our dream, and to make sure nothing like that ever happened to someone again."

Well, now what do you say to that? None of us knew. This was either all one big fucked up joke, or fantasy and horror just got really real. The signs were there, though. I couldn't deny it. He wasn't lying.

"Borris, I'm so sorry!" Brendolyn broke the silence first.

"It's okay. It was five years ago. I'm just glad I was there to protect you. And he's gone now, so you have nothing to worry about," he reassured her.

"They're dogs, so once they pick up your scent, he wasn't going to stop until he had his way with you. It's partly why I had to kill him. And also, for my sister."

"So is it safe for us to return to camp now that he's dead?" Melissa asked. Borris hesitated.

"Give it a night. One night, and then you can return."

"Why one night? What are we going to eat or sleep on?" I asked. It was probably not the best time to think about trying to catch some z's, but I needed to know when my next nap would be. This shit was exhausting.

"Because I'll know where you are. Willy never traveled alone. He traveled in a pack. And once his followers realize their alpha is dead, I'm dinner. I can't have you around for that. I'll be able to lead them away from here, so you're all safe. By morning, if the wolves are still out, you'll know I'm dead. But they're all the same. They're not going to stop until everyone here is either dead or a part of their pack. Unless I kill them first."

Rage was in his eyes. He was thirsty for a hunt and it was terrifying. The trauma he went through, I'm not surprised. But holy fuck, he wasn't kidding.

"Stay here. It was nice meeting you ladies. Lena, I'm sorry. It's a full moon, the music is loud, and tonight, I hunt."

And he was off. Just like that. He just ran the fuck away back towards the festival. Now it was dark. We could only see from the silver glow of the moon. I looked up at it. He was right. It was full. I heard howling in the distance. I tried to ignore it and tell myself I was just hearing things and it was all in my head. But Melissa looked wigged the fuck out, and Brendolyn grabbed my arm and clung to me tight, so I knew it wasn't just in my head.

"I just wanted to be a part of music history by coming to this big show," Brendolyn said.

"I think you're a part of history alright. Just one that's about to have a very ugly ending," Melissa affirmed.

CHAPTER 15

Chapter Song

"Manic" by Wage War

For the remainder of the night we sat in darkness, in silence, in the elements. We could hear the howls and growls, and the music playing loud. At least we could hear the show we were missing once again echo through the trees. I didn't know what Borris's big plan was to eliminate the beasts, but it sounded like it wasn't working.

"How do you think Borris is?" I asked.

"Probably long gone," Melissa said.

"If we were at camp, I could be charging my rocks and reading the cards in this moonlight. It might be able to help us figure out what's going on," Brendolyn said. I would argue that her hippy voodoo stuff was a bunch of hocus pocus, but after the week we've all had, who the fuck knows.

"How do the bands not notice the werewolves in the crowds every night? It sounds like they're multiplying," I wondered.

"Who knows. Maybe it's all in our heads, and the noises we think we keep hearing are just regular wolves. In these woods," Melissa tried to reason.

"But Borris," I started to say, but she interrupted me.

"Borris is full of shit. He's been an odd ball ever since we met him. How do you know he didn't just make that whole story up to scare you? He probably just figured we were too weird for his liking and made it all up to leave our group and meet new people."

She had a point. That did make more sense than the whole dying to save us thing. Fucker, probably took my dream and decided I was too fucked up and played in to the whole werewolf thing to get out.

"Except, I know what I saw!" Brendolyn interjected.

"How? You said so yourself, you were stuffed in a box, and you thought you were being trafficked. Honestly, that's probably all it was. That's the real horror of this world. Sex trafficking. Not werewolves."

"You weren't even there!" Brendolyn was clearly annoyed. She doesn't like being told she was wrong. Especially when it's something she's sure she experienced.

"It's no use trying to argue with her. It's just her way of coping with all of this. She's not going to reason with you," I said, in some kind of hopes of comforting my friend.

"Look, we don't know what's going on. All we know is what we think we experienced, and what Borris told us. But yes, Melissa, you're right, Borris is a stranger. A stranger who may have made it all up, but his body language sure was convincing. Are werewolves real? I don't fucking know! But I do know that I don't want to find out. So, to play it safe. Let's just stay here until the birds wake up, and then we can go back to our camp and get cleaned up and make the most of what's left of this music festival." Everyone agreed, and we dropped the subject for the remainder of the night.

CHAPTER 16

Chapter Song:

"Crazy Bitch" by Buckcherry

We tried resting our eyes for the remainder of the night, but that all ended when the birds started chirping. We all woke up. It was quiet. The sun was coming up, and the nightly chaos was dying down.

"Well, if we can't beat them, we might as well join them. I'm tired of hiding out. So what if they're possible werewolves, or if they're just drugged out festival folk. They're up all night partying, and they sleep all day. So that's been keeping us up all night, so let's just sleep for the day. I came here to have an epic time. So fuck it. I'm heading back to camp. I'm going to get a solid 5 hours of sleep in, and then I'm going to rock and rage!" Brendolyn had a point. We spent a lot of money and time planning for this trip. I'm not a big partier like her. I'm pretty happy standing in the back listening to the music and taking pictures. But I haven't even done much of that so far, and there's still a bunch of awesome bands set to perform before the week is over. "Alright, I'm in. But if shit gets too weird, don't be surprised if I just peace out and head back to camp," I said.

"I wouldn't expect it any other way from you. I'm just glad you're willing to give it a try!" Brendolyn smiled.

"See this is what I've been trying to say. We're getting too caught up in our heads over things instead of just enjoying the festival. Of course weird stuff is going to happen. We're camping out among dehydrated hippies on Molly. I'd be concerned if they weren't howling like wolves," Melissa chimed in. It's not what she's been saying, but there's no sense arguing with her. We just let her have her moment.

"Well, I'm fucking beat. This night felt like an eternity. Let's see what's left of our camp and get some sleep," I decided.

We all found our way back out of the woods and over to our campsite. Most of the camps were pretty trashed. Ours seemed fine, but it looked like Borris helped himself to food and supplies. The cooler was locked up, but a lot of the water and food was gone. I don't think we ate that much.

"Where'd all the food and water go?" Melissa asked, also noticing it being pretty picked over.

"Borris most likely the damn moocher. He better not have taken my cheddar stuffed hot dogs!" Brendolyn grumbled. I took a look.

"He did. But he left you one," I said while handing it to her. She snatched it out of my hand and started chomping on it.

"Don't you want to heat that over a fire?" Melissa asked.

"No. I like them raw." Melissa grimaced. "I know. It's weird. Just let it go. I've gotten used to it by now," I said to Melissa. Brendolyn has always preferred her hotdogs fresh out of the package, but yet claims she doesn't like bologna. Makes zero sense.

We all grabbed a snack and ate sparingly because we didn't bring money to buy every meal. It's literally why we packed all the food that we did. So now we're all on rations. After our snack, I hit the sack. Brendolyn and Melissa joined in too. We sealed up the tent real good and snoozed away. This time without the horrible nightmares.

Brendolyn woke up first, which is very unlike her. For as much as I like naps, she could sleep for days. I suffer from insomnia, so I usually just don't sleep. Which is why I was so surprised to hear how long I'd slept the day before from Borris. I swear my body was under a sleeping spell or something to get that much sleep in without waking up once.

I heard Brendolyn wrestling in her duffle bag, pulling shit out, and then the tent unzipped. I figured she went to go take a shower. She returned after some time. Her hair was wet and in braids. I sat up and decided, I should do the same. I grabbed some clothes, a towel, and shower shoes and went to get washed up. I came back, and Melissa was getting ready to do the same.

By the time we all got cleaned up and put on fresh concert clothes, there was a big crowd heading to the main stage from the camping area. "Must be time for one of the big names to start," I said.

"Do we know who?" Brendolyn asked.

"No clue. We lost the map with the itinerary," Melissa replied.

"Well, I guess we should just follow the crowd and find out!" Brednolyn said. She grabbed a White Claw Surge out of the cooler and put it in her fanny pack. Then she offered them to Melissa and me. We both declined, because it's still fucking hot and we were out of water. So she shrugged, and put a second one in her pocket and opened a third.

"How many of those are you planning on drinking?" I asked.

"Just this one. The others are for you two in case you change your mind. And if you don't, it saves me money from buying beer from a vendor and energy from walking back to camp to get one." She's always thinking.

"So, we ready to party hardy?!" She asked excited to see what this day will bring us.

"I'm as ready as I'll ever be," I said.

"Yep. Let's go," Melissa said.

Brendolyn happily led the way to wherever it was that all the others were going. We figured that would be our best tactic now that we don't have our map and itinerary anymore. The masses of people are likely going to be where the best shows are happening at any given moment.

We followed the crowd to a big warehouse looking building where a lot of the rave-type things happen. We hadn't ventured over this way yet, because that's not really much of our style. But at this point, it's about all there was to do from the looks of the empty stages we passed along the way.

There were a bunch of zoomers and zoomer wanna-be's in line to get in. They were all wearing their middle parts and space buns, dressed half naked and thinking they invented the y2k new millennium look. I rolled my eyes at the girls with the light up binkies, and minded by business in line.

I pulled out my noise balancing earbuds and popped some vertigo meds, because I could tell by the music echoes off the hollow metal and concrete structure, this was going to be a doozy if I didn't.

We finally got to the entrance, linked arms, as to not get separated in the chaos, and walked inside. I was immediately blinded by a green neon light shining in my face and foam soaking through my shoes. We trudged our way through and looked for somewhere to go that wasn't in the middle of everyone pushing their way in. It was too loud to try and have a conversation, so we just stuck together and made the most of it. That's really what you gotta do in these situations to begin with. We're not rookies, so we have an unspoken system down. Melissa is tall, so she stays in the back. Brendolyn is pushy, so she leads the group. And I'm fragile, yet protective, so I keep people in check when they try to break up our train chain.

Brendolyn led us to a spot off to the side where there weren't as many people, and the laser beams weren't flying around to burn our corneas. This is when I was finally able to get a look around and scope out the scene.

"Holy fuck, what did we walk into?!" I asked in disbelief.

I scanned the room. There were people and hairy people well, humping and swapping partners all over the floor. While others were ignoring what was happening and practically trampling on them to try and dance. Legitimately, it wasn't one or two, the middle of the floor was covered in naked bodies.

"Orgy," Melissa confirmed. No shit Sherlock. I know that.

"Wolf-human orgy," Brendolyn clarified.

"I don't think this is our scene," I said.

"Speak for yourself! If you can't beat 'em, join 'em!" Brendolyn half jokingly exclaimed. Then she ran into the middle of the fuck fest and started dancing with strangers.

"At least the music is good," I mentioned to Melissa.

"Yeah, there's that," She said. We stayed to the side and bobbed our heads to the deafening beat. We both kept our eye on Brendolyn, because well, she has a foot wound that's about to get trench foot in this nasty foam and semon swamp we're standing in, and she almost died last night. I don't know how she just bounces back after a night like that, but she did.

I wondered if this was how the beasts were multiplying. Maybe they were just making more human-dogs in this warehouse. I didn't mention it to Melissa though because she's convinced herself that we're being illogical. I don't know what she thinks is happening on the orgy floor, but people can be pretty hairy I suppose.

It was pretty interesting to watch though. Almost like a drugged out sex ballet. At one point everyone synced up to the beat of the music; the dancing, humping, moaning, and howling alike. The wolves had their claws out. It didn't look like they were out to kill, more like maybe they came out in arousal. I'm clearly not a wolf or a dog or cat, so I don't know how that works. I was also getting pretty uncomfortable just standing there watching like a creep. But there was nothing else to do, and it was like watching a train wreck. I couldn't look away.

Brendolyn came skipping back to us after a few songs. Only she had a small posse following her. "Hey! I made friends!" She happily announced.

"I see that. Hi, I'm Lena. This is Melissa," I introduced us. The posse smiled and looked at us wide-eyed. Yep. They're on some psychedelic shit.

"Melissa, you look like a mushroom!" One said.

"Woah! Just like the Toad in Mario!" another agreed.

"Thank you?" Melissa took what seemed to be a compliment, but also was sort of insulting.

"Right on! So like, where's Luigi?" A dumb looking blonde asked.

"We don't have a Luigi," I said. The shock of the news instantly brought her to tears, "But he's my favorite," she wailed.

"Yeah, yeah. Me too. So sorry for our misfortune," I said.

"Are you ready to go? I'm pretty thirsty," Brendolyn said to Melissa and me. I thought she'd never get tired of this place.

"Yeah. Let's go," I said, and linked our arms.

"We're gunna stay and party some more Frost Byte. I've been eyeing that hairy hottie and wanna take him for a ride on the foam floor," one of the posse said to Brendolyn.

"Okay! Have fun! Bye!" She waved and we made our way to the door.

"Did he just call you Frost Byte?" I asked.

"Yeah. They said I needed a festival name. And called me Frost Byte. I don't know. I just went with it," she answered.

"Well, okay then," I accepted.

"That was an experience I wish I never had and will forever be burned in my brain," Melissa mentioned once we got out of the warehouse.

"Same," I agreed.

"Yeah. I tried to ignore the weird stuff and make the most of it. But it was hard to do when you're trying not to step on people's special parts while dancing," Brendolyn cringed. Yep. It was weird.

"I think I need to go take another shower," I said as we made our way through the field of stages.

CHAPTER 17

Chapter Song

"Livin' On The Edge" by Aerosmith

We washed up and changed into clean clothes and footwear, and started talking about what we wanted to eat, now that most of the food was gone.

"Okay, so we have like 3 and a half days left of the festival. Food stands are outrageously priced. So how much money do we have, and how much food do we have?" Brendolyn was breaking it down, trying to find a way to make the resources we had last the rest of the festival. We took a thorough inventory and discussed meals we could make with what we had left, and how we could use the money we had to buy items that would contribute to meals we'd make at the camp.

"So, if we buy two sausage sandwiches for $20, We can cut up the sausage into smaller pieces, and put it over rice. We can break the buns in half, so we each get some bread. The peppers and onions can go over the rice too. But we'll keep it all separate, that way there should be enough left over, so we can use the veggies in another meal as well, like a soup or something," Brendolyn said. The woman had a plan.

"What about water to make the rice though? Borris took all our water," Melissa pointed out.

"There's free water in the barrels," I suggested.

"It's poison. If the water was any good, Borris wouldn't have bothered with taking our water here. I think that’s what’s turning people into the monsters,” Brendolyn insisted.

“Well, if it's a bacteria, it’ll die after boiling the water, which we will have to do to make the rice in the first place,” Melissa reasoned. Brendolyn hesitated. She was really reluctant to use the water.

“Do you think there’s a stream or a crick anywhere nearby? In the woods maybe?” She asked.

“We don’t know. We don’t have a map,” I said.

“But that’s not a bad idea. There might be berries or something in those woods we can use to eat too,” Melissa added.

“And if they’re ‘never wakeup’ berries? We’re dead,” I reminded her how none of us actually know anything about living off of the land.

We sat in silence as we thought about what we should do. "Wasn't there rice with those kabobs you said you ate?" Brendolyn asked me.

"Yeah there was," I said. "It was like $15 for that though. We don't have enough.

"No, but maybe they'll just give us a bowl of rice cheaper," she countered.

"It's worth a shot. I'll go find out," I said, and got up to walk down to the food stands to see what we could swindle.

To my surprise they gave me a quart of rice for $5. I figured that'd be enough to hold us over. While I was at it, I went and grabbed the sausage sandwiches too.

"So for $25, I got us supplies for dinner," I announced upon my return back to camp.

"Great! Melissa got the fire started," Brendolyn said. I wasn't sure what we needed the fire for at this point since we literally just bought dinner, but I wasn't going to question it.

We divided up the food into three bowls. A shallow bed of rice, topped with some sausage, peppers, and onions, and a quarter of a bun. It was pretty delicious too. We ended up with enough left over for each of us to either have seconds, or another meal. Given our trying times, we all decided to save the leftovers for another meal.

"Do you think we could sell our mushrooms and oregano to dummies and convince them it's weed and shrooms?" Brendolyn brought up.

"Maybe, but I don't like the legal repercussions that would come with that if we were caught and shit," I pointed out. Given the fact that we weren't dumb 18 year olds, but grown adults with careers like in the law, and news, and education.

"Right. Well, it was a thought," she said, but agreed that none of us are willing to lose our jobs for a few extra bucks. Even if we'd likely get away with it, it wasn't worth the risk.

We hung out by the fire for a while after cleaning up from dinner, just talking and enjoying each other's company. It seemed like most of the time we were all on this trip we were so distracted by the chaos, and Borris's antics, that we didn't have much time actually bonding and doing the things we came here to do. It was a good night to reset and carry on like normal. Melissa started to get restless when the roar of the crowd picked up.

"Who do you think is on the main stage tonight?" she asked. I shrugged.

"Let's go check it out. It's gotta be someone good," Brendolyn chimed in.

"Alright," I said and stood up and got ready to head back out into the crowd. We put the fire out, and geared up with all our usual things, and headed towards the heart of the venue.
"Let's Rock!" I said.

"Let's Roll!" Melissa added.

"Let's Get Outta Control!" Brendolyn said to finish our chant.

CHAPTER 18

Chapter Song

"I Won't" by AJR

We party rocked the night away. I even stayed up the whole time. And it was a blast. We just stayed together, did our thing, and ignored the fact that half the crowd looked like something out of a sci-fi film.

As the night was nearing an end, I noticed that sci-fi looking crowd seemed to be in the majority. I didn't know where they were coming from, but they were either getting real comfortable in their own skin, or they were multiplying by the hour. To my surprise, they didn't seem aggressive though. Instead, they looked a little lost and confused, like no one told them they were a wolfin until this very night.

Looking around at all the beasts, I was reminded of the night before. If Borris was right, we're all gonners.

"I don't think Borris' plan, whatever it was, worked," I said to Brendolyn. I knew she'd understand more so than Miss-In-Denial behind me. Brendolyn looked at me sad, realizing what I hadn't put together yet. She hugged me tight.

"The annoying bastard is gone gone isn't he?" I asked.

She nodded, "I think so."

"Well that's a buzz kill," I said.

"You aren't even drinking," Brendolyn reminded me.

"I know. But it did kill the mood." She hugged me again. I guess the fucker made some sort of impact on our trip. Damn him.

The rest of the night I was in a weird funk. I was listening to the music, and genuinely enjoying it, but I just couldn't bring myself to rock on like I normally would have. Not that my version of 'rocking on' is much wilder than standing and listening to the music in the first place. I gave a few claps of applause when appropriate, and bobbed my head a bit, but that was about all I had in me. My mind was too distracted with thoughts of everything else. *How is everyone here just fine with what's been going on? Why aren't the bands addressing the extra hairy audience, or the fact that I'm pretty sure they're all hanging out backstage? What happened to Borris? The man stormed into our lives, saved two of our lives, and then just dumped a bunch of trauma on us and peaced the fuck out; taking our food and water with him. Bastard.* I was still pretty mad about that. And at the same time, there was a sinking sense of worry in the pit of my stomach. Something just wasn't right. I felt jaded; faded. I needed to clear my head.

I looked over at Brendolyn, who was clapping and bopping away. I reached over and grabbed the drink of hard seltzer out of her hand and took a swig. She looked over at me, smiled, read my thoughts through my eyes and said, "Keep it. It's giving me a headache anyway." I nodded as if to say 'thank you'. She gets me. I like that about her.

By the time the night ended, I was ready for bed. We got back to camp, and Melissa sat and reviewed all the photos and videos she took throughout the night. Being tall has its advantages, like being able to see the stage well enough to take decent pictures. I got ready for bed and crashed. Brendolyn sat up with Melissa and helped her decide which pictures were worth keeping, posting, and deleting. Then I assume they went to bed too.

My insomnia came back. I was half asleep, half awake the whole night/morning. No dreaming happened at least, which I was a bit thankful for that part, but at the same time, I did not feel rested at all when I woke up the next day. When I finally got up, Brendolyn was no where to be found, and my head was pounding like a Mother fucker. I desperately needed water.

CHAPTER 19

Chapter Song

"Madness" by Muse

******Picks up where Chapter 1 Left Off******

While my mind was off in a daze replaying everything that happened this week, Brendolyn guided us back to camp, and she pulled out the emergency snacks she had stashed away.

"I can't believe this place got so trashed while we were out at the show last night," I say as I stuff a mini chocolate chip cookie in my mouth.

"Yeah, I don't remember us leaving the cooler unlocked. We've been pretty good at keeping everything secure here, especially with everything that's been going on. The beasts are hungry buggers for sure," Brendolyn remarks.

"No. We didn't leave it unlocked. I remember watching Melissa close it all up while we were sitting by the fire. How did they break in?" Now I'm starting to get pissed.

Brendolyn shrugs. She doesn't know any more than I know. Then it dawns on me, "You don't think," I stop mid sentence.

"What?" Brendolyn asks, encouraging me to complete my thought.

"What are the chances Borris is still alive? He stole from us once already. He's the only one other than the three of us who knew where we kept the food and how to get into it."

"I don't know. Maybe. I don't know how he would have survived the wolves though. Unless, he chickened out and has just been hiding out since he left." She has a point. There's no way he would have survived. But there are a shit ton of wolves now. More than he may have anticipated. He very well could have just decided to lay low.

"Maybe. He was pretty fired up when he bolted the other night though," I say. I really just can't see how the Borris who was so fixated on avenging his sister's death for five years would just back down.

"Unless, they turned him into one of them," Brendolyn suggests.

"Could be. We still don't even really know how you get turned into one of them. Maybe he ran out of our water and drank the water from the barrels."

"Maybe, but he took a lot of water with him. I doubt he ran out that fast." She has a point.

"Yeah, I don't know. I guess I just hope he's okay." I hate to think something bad happened to him.
"Me too. Speaking of which, I also hope Melissa is okay. I thought maybe she circled back to our camp when we lost her in the stampede," Brendolyn points out.

"Maybe we should go look for her." I'd hate to lose her to this mess too. How would we explain that when we don't bring her home? Or if she returns as a werewolf?

"Yeah, maybe we should," Brendolyn agrees. I peek out from our tent to see if the coast is clear. It's not. Beasts are ransacking the next campsite over from us. If they catch our scent, we're next.

"We gotta wait this one out a bit. Beastie boys are right next door."

"Shit. Well looks like we're staying in here for a while. Hopefully Melissa went to find help, or maybe the bathroom, or something," Brendolyn is trying to reason with herself. "We'll go look when it's safer to step out of this tent." I agree with her. It's hide out time right now.

"I feel like I'm going bonkers. Straight mad like Alice and the hatter," I say breaking the silence.

"What are you going bonkers over?" Brendolyn asks.

"I don't know. I can't help it. I'm angry with myself for getting us all in this mess. We should have shut Borris down day one when he tried to join our group. I should have told him to fuck off and find friends somewhere else. Because now his memory is living rent free in my brain, and I don't like it. He's fucking confusing," I vent. It's been on my mind ever since the night he left.

"Well, we can't change the past. Maybe he's okay. We don't know. All we know is he helped us when we needed it. Who knows where we'd be right now if we had told him to fuck off." She has a point. We'd be dead for sure by now.

"Yeah. I just hate how he acted like a nice guy. He followed me when I ran away in my sleep. He was there and listened to me go on and on about my delusional and terrifying dream. We had a moment. I almost cared about him. And then he saved you. And then he unloaded what was going on and about his sister and shit, and he left. He stole our stuff, which is a dick move, and we're likely not going to see him again. And I don't know if I like him or hate him. I'm still conflicted. I usually have a good sense of judgment on people, but this one I haven't figured out yet. I fear it might be too late. Should we have gone after him? Should we be looking for his body too? Or is he still alive and still stealing our food? I don't fucking know! And I'm pissed about it!"

Brendolyn isn't saying anything now. I think she's waiting to make sure I'm done, or she's processing.

"You had a moment?" she asks. Out of all the shit I just said, that's what she fixates on? Ugh! Typical.

"Yeah," I reluctantly admit. I know where this is going now. She grins widely, "Spill!"

"All the other stuff I had to say and this is what you want to know about?" I protest.

"We'll circle back to the heavy stuff in a minute. But yes. Right now, you're telling me about this moment you had with Borris! I need all the deets!"

I sigh. She's not going to let this go until I tell her. "Well it was the other night. I had a nightmare and sleep walked to Timbuktu. Borris followed me. I guess I woke him up and he was concerned. So we ended up talking for a while, and he was telling me about how he loves Blink-182 and always wanted to be on stage and shit but never performed the songs for anyone. So I let him do it for me. And he sang some corny Blink song and said it was his way of trying to tell me he liked me or some shit. And then we kissed. And that was pretty much it. I got hungry, and we got up to go find food."

Smiling from ear to ear, Brendolyn is beyond thrilled to have heard this story. "Awe! You like him! He likes you! He left his mark on your heart, not your brain. That's why you're so worried! Okay. So, once it's safe, we're going to find Melissa, we'll quickly fill her in, and then we're finding Borris. Dead or alive. You need closure."

"I don't know about all of that. There's a good chance I'm just going to crack him one in the gonads."

Brendolyn shrugs, "Well, that's fine. He deserves it." At least she's reasonable enough to recognize this hasn't been a bed of roses.

CHAPTER 20

Chapter Song:

"Wanted, Dead or Alive" by Bon Jovi

About 20 minutes or so pass by, and it's finally quiet. I peak outside, the coast is clear.

"Alright, looks like it's time to find Melissa, and go off on a man hunt!" I announce. Brendolyn jumps up, full-sized backpack full of supplies this time, and is armed and ready to go.

We quietly creep out of the tent. I make sure to close it up nice and securely. We had plenty of time to game plan while we waited for the dogs to leave. We're looking for any signs of life, places to hide out, or places to stock up on life sustaining items.

First stop, bathrooms and shower houses. I checked the women's, Brendolyn covered the men's. We found nothing. Now we're off to the food vendors to traumatically relive my dream. Some are closed up because they've either run out of food, or were ransacked by the hungry beasts. Others are still operational, and still overpriced. We opt to inspect the ones that are vacant.

"Nothing but crusty burritos," Brendolyn says, defeated after searching the taco truck.

"All I found were roaches in that one," I cringe as I gesture towards the cheesesteak shack I just came from.

Now that we've searched the sanitation stations, and the

nourishment nests, it's time to try the stages and merch tents.

"For the sake of time, do we want to split up?" Brendolyn offers. I'm hesitant.

"I do, but at the same time, I don't, because what if something happens?"

"Good point. Okay, where do you want to try next, the stages or merch?"

"I think we might have better luck finding Melissa at the merch tents."

"Okay, then we're off!" Brendolyn declares, and leads me in that direction.

As we walk to that part of the venue, I keep my eyes peeled. I can't help but think we're missing something. We get to the line of merchandise tents. They're organized by band, and are insanely expensive. For the most part, these are all still operational. I guess King Capital needs his money.

We look in each tent and act like creeps bending over to see if anyone is hiding under the tables. People likely just assume we're high and dismiss our odd behavior.
"Where the hell is Melissa?" I ask. I'm getting frustrated.

"I don't know. Let's just see if maybe she's watching a band at one of the stages," Brendolyn decides. It's the last place to really look. The problem is, the stages are scattered all over the venue grounds. We have no map, so we can't even narrow it down based on which bands are at which stages.

"I'm ready to give up," Brendolyn says in defeat after we finished searching five stages.

"Pst, guys!" Someone whispers from under a broken stage. I look in that direction, fully expecting to find nothing considering I'm delusional at this point, but to my surprise, it's Melissa!

"What the Hell are you doing down there?!" I shout.

"Shhh! Get down! I have intel!" Melissa whispers. Brendolyn and I crouch down to her level and army crawl under the stage.

"Okay, first, I'm okay! I saw you guys looking for me, but I couldn't come out in the open. They're after me," Melissa begins to explain.

"Who is?" I ask.

"The wolves. When the stampede came through and we got separated, it's because I panicked and ran into the herd instead of away from the herd. One bit me, and now it's hunting for my scent."

"So you're a believer now?" Brendolyn states. I punch her. Now is not the time for her sass. "Ow! Sorry. I'm glad you're okay. How did you get away?"

"Borris snatched me up like Tarzan and took me here. He's still alive! He's been in hiding. He told me it's not safe for me to follow him, or to be out in the open."

"Do you believe him?" I ask.

"I don't know. It's odd that he's always been conveniently there to save us from these things. But at the same time, I have no reason not to believe him." She makes a valid point.

"Well now what?" Brendolyn asks.

"Now, we find Borris and demand some answers," I say. I'm kinda pissed at him. He's clearly the one who keeps taking our food, and that's not oaky. If he had just asked, we would have sent him away with a hefty care package, but he didn't. He chose to be sneaky, and I don't trust that.

"I'm staying here for now," Melissa says.

"Do you want Lena or me to stay here with you?" Brendolyn asks. She doesn't like when we get separated.

"No. I think if someone is going after Borris, you shouldn't go alone. He seems to attract trouble. I'm okay here for now." Reluctantly, Brendolyn and I agree. We leave her with extra bandages for her bite wound, and some snacks to get her by.

CHAPTER 21

Chapter Song

"Kill or Be Killed" by Muse

"He's gotta be hiding out in the woods somewhere," I mention, "It's the only logical place.

"Or back stage of the main stage," Brendolyn counters.

"Why there? If he's hiding from them, and that's where they're staying, then he'd be an idiot to be there."

"Right. But he might be spying on them to try and sneak attack his kill."

"Okay, that's a good point. But I don't want to go there if we don't have to. I'm not trying to get us killed," I say. So we head into the woods.

We walk through the woods a while, looking into the trees, on the ground for foot prints, just about any sign of life that could point to Borris.

"At least we know he's not dead," Brendolyn breaks the silence.

"So we think. Just because he was alive when Melissa saw him, doesn't mean he's still alive," I point out.

We've been searching for what seems like hours. I'm glad we found Melissa. I was really worried about that. But it's starting to turn to dusk, I'm getting hungry, and we haven't seen a trace of Borris all day. If it weren't for my rage, I'd give up.

I sigh in defeat, "Okay, let's check backstage before the big show starts. We're clearly not finding him here."

"Okay. Let's check back on Melissa first. See how she's doing and if she's feeling up to join us," Brendolyn says, "A throuple is better than a couple after all."

I roll my eyes at her cheeky grin. "You see what I did there?" She says, so proud of herself.

"Yes, I get it," I reply.

We make our way back to Melissa's stage, only to find she isn't there.

"Well fuck. She's either in the bathroom, back at camp, or she's been killed," I say.

"Yes, because those are the only three logical explanations as to where she could be," Brendolyn says.

"Yep! Right now, yes it is. That's all I have the mental capacity for today."

"Okay then. We'll go with those three options and hope it's not the killed one."

"Thank you."

So now we have to go backstage, just the two of us. This ought to be fun. We're almost at the entrance, and Brendolyn pulls out self-defense weapons. They look like ordinary things, but open up into blades and other stabby things. I doubt these actually stand a fighting chance against what we're about to face, but I supposed something is better than nothing. I take the one that looks like a tiger and put it in my pocket. We take a deep breath, lock arms, and head on in.

CHAPTER 22

Chapter Song

"Welcome to the Circus" by Five Finger Death Punch

No sooner do we get through security (we invested in backstage passes, that we never took advantage of until now), are we met with chaos. Naturally everyone is getting warmed up and ready for the big show tonight. Roadies and groupies alike are scattered all through the backstage and practice stage area. Most of the bands are likely in their prospective dressing rooms.

We push through the group of fangirls, and search for anything that would resemble a wolf's den, or a crazed out Borris den. Brendolyn sees something, grabs my arms and picks up the pace. She's like a dog who spotted the mailman. I let her lead the way and ask no questions. She pulls me behind a tall case that likely holds one of the big ass speakers. We hide. She peers around the case, looks around, and pulls out her mini dagger. She looks at me, puts her pointer finger over her lips to remind me to be quiet, and gestures to my weapon. I pull it out, at the ready.

Brendolyn sneaks across the way towards the back of the practice stage. I stealthily follow. She then lunges towards what I thought was a furry bean bag chair. She jumps on it and starts slicing it with her blade.

The bean bag chair stands up. It's alive! Brendolyn is now on what I think is its back. Her arm wrapped around its front. She slices across what would be its neck. I cringe and look away. I do not want to get sick. The hairy monster moans. It slams my wife up against a wall. *Shit. Time to intervene.*

I jump in, and stab the 'Cousin It' on steroids in the leg region. I think it was a knee cap. Monster man didn't like that. But I stab again. In the foot this time. I have no idea why we're doing this, but we started this mess, time to finish it. Brendolyn runs off, leaving me to beat its ass on my own. I'm doing my best. It's hard to effectively wound something so thick and meaty with a weapon so small and stabby.

A quiet *BANG* goes off. The beast wails. Its arms wrap around its head and falls to the ground. It slithers into the darkness backstage. I turn and see Brendolyn putting a pistol in her boot.

"What the fuck was that?!" I insist.

"Shhhh. I saw this when we walked in. I went to retrieve it. It's the only way to get rid of the beasts," She explains.

"What? How do you know?"

"It's how I was able to get away earlier, before the mob came after us for revenge. I didn't kill him. I just dismantled its Jekyll and Hyde abilities. Watch."

I look over to where the monster siddled away. Moments go by, and a lad emerges. It's BORRIS?!

"BORRIS?! What the Fuck?!" I have no idea what is happening. I'm straight shook.

He's all cut up and bloodied. He reaches around and covers the back of his head.

"Yeah, you got me pretty good," he says with a smug look on his face.

"What the hell happened?! Did they turn you?!" I'm still trying to put the pieces together.

"What? No. I mean, they did, but years ago," He explains.

"YEARS AGO?! Explain," I demand, then turn to Brendolyn, "and how did you know that was Borris?"

Brendolyn jumps in to answer first, "When he was wrestling with Willy, and told me to run, I thought I saw him puff out into a beast, but I wasn't sure at the time. I was in shock, and it was all a blur, and I didn't get a good look. But when we came back here today, it all came flooding back to me. I saw him huddled up sleeping, and recognized his markings. I took a gamble."

"That checks out. Okay. Now, traitor. Explain what the fuck is going on."

"Well, I'm not a bad guy. I do care about all of you, and I did save your lives. You weren't supposed to be here. I didn't want you to know. I didn't want you to see me like this. But here it goes, I'm a werewolf. It happened the summer my sister died. It's the music. The low vibrations in the music is what's growing the mob. It's all part of a greater plan to destroy and conquer. They killed my sister. I got my revenge on Willy. He raped my sister and he's the reason why she's dead today. It's his pack that started all of this. So I've been following the pack, acting like I didn't see what happened to my sister. Show after show, we grow bigger, and stronger. I built my way up to Beta wolf. That is, until I killed Willy. That wolf that got you, Dolly, he was a decoy. A newbie in training. It was easy for you to kill him. He was young."

"So what's your plan? Where do you sit in all of this?" Brendolyn asked.

Borris smirked, "Oh, you'll just have to wait and see for the grand finale."

Borris turns around and runs off into the dark shadows of the back of the practice stage. We run after him, but for a wounded wolf, he's still pretty quick. We lost sight of him.

"Well now what?" I ask.
At this moment, fireworks go off, and the crowd roars. The show is beginning.

"Let's go see where the hell Melissa is and wait for the grand finale, I guess. I don't know, I'm out of ideas."

CHAPTER 23

Chapter Song

"Werewolf" by Motionless in White

Brendolyn leads the way back to the old stage Melissa was under the last time we saw her. We just hope that maybe she returned, and is alive and well. Everything is so fucked up right now.

"So, if Melissa knew Borris is still alive, do you think she knows he's a werewolf?" I ask.

"I don't know. I don't know how the wolf reveal thing works. I thought it was just at the full moon, but that seems to not be how these music wolves work."

"Wait. If the music is what's turning people into wolves, then maybe it's the music that's bringing the wolf out of people at night." I think I'm talking in circles now. "And how have we not turned yet?"

"Well, we haven't been that involved in the music as much as a lot of the others I think. Plus you have your noise canceling earbuds. I bet they might help deflect from the vibrations that make people wolf out. And I don't know about me or Melissa. I know my hearing just sucks, so that could very well be helping in my favor," Brendolyn suggested. We don't really know the answers. It's all just speculation at this point.

We get to the stage and look for Melissa. "She's back!" Brendolyn exclaims and starts army crawling under the stage. She lets out a scream and backs the fuck back out from under the stage.

"She's a wolf!" *Well, looks like she's not immune to the music after all.*

"Fuck! Melissa, cover your ears! De-wolf De-Wolf!" I yell at her, trying to get her to realize what's happening and turn back.

She snarls, showing her fangs like an angry beast.

"Melissa! For fucks sake! It's me, Jelena!"

BANG! Goes the bullet out of the gun Brendolyn stole. Melissa yelped and went back under the stage. We watch as she morphs back into her original form.

"What the hell happened?!" I asked.

"I turned into a wolf. Borris found me. He told me to hide here, and he would protect me. It's no use. We're all either going to turn into a wolf and end up as puppy chow. I've been guarding the den with the pups. There are so many who are turning to wolves by the minute. Song by song. Borris, explained everything. We all have a choice to make. To join them, or be finished by them. I chose to join them. You should too. Nobody's leaving this place alive."

"What? Where's the den you're guarding?" Brendolyn asks.

"Under the stage. There's a hole that leads to Hell. Big, red, hot, den of Hell. It's where the pups are staying to learn how to control their new abilities. Borris has been working with me to help me get stronger faster. I recommend you go see tonight's show to find out your fate."

"What the Hell Melissa this aint you!" I argue. She would never do something like this. I'm in utter disbelief.

"Yeah, well, it's me now, Lena. Sorry 'bout it." She lets out a loud *AHOOOOOO* and a chorus of small howls echo from beneath the stage. She wasn't kidding. I bent to look below the stage and there it was, a gaping portal to hell, full of its hounds.

"You better run," Melissa says with a snarl, hunger gleaming in her eyes. We run towards the crowd, hoping to lose them among all the people.

Melissa and the young wolves are quick on our tails. They're babies, so they're faster, stronger, hungrier, thirstier; basically we're screwed.

"The water! It's not making people turn into wolves! We CAN drink it!" Brendolyn exclaims mid run.

"Okay, great! Now's not the time!"

"Right. Sorry. I've just been so thirsty!"

"Yeah, same here. But if we stop now, we're dog food."

We get deep in the middle of the crowd. We know exactly what to do. We start the mosh pit.

CHAPTER 24

Chapter Song

"Riot" by Three Days Grace

If there's one thing a group of rock festival goers love, it's a good mosh pit. We just keep it going and work on expanding it, big and strong. The bands on stage love it too. They're crowd surfing, and jumping off of amps. Now it's a rock show!

You really have to watch in these. You can get really hurt. But it's perfect for now. The wolves are getting lost in the pit. They don't know up from down or left from right. I saw one crowd surfing and howling all the while. It's a great distraction. Let the pups play.

Brendolyn and I elbow our way back out of the pit after we got the whole crowd involved. We met back up by the food vendors and suck down some of the nasty water.

"That ought to hold them for a while," Brendolyn says as we exchange a high-five.

"Yeah, I hope so," I say, keeping my eyes peeled for Melissa or Borris. I see her slip through security to the back stage.

"Well would you look at that. Melissa just went backstage. What do you think they're up to now?" I ask.

"I don't know, but I bet it has something to do with whatever Borris has planned for the grand finale."

"We have to try to stop whatever it is from happening," I say.

"Okay, and how do we do that? You and I are not athletic. We're lucky I have good aim with a gun, but this thing doesn't have that many bullets left in it. I don't think that's going to help."

She's right. I have no idea what we could ever do to stop whatever it is that's supposed to happen from happening. Then I remember Woodstock of '99.

"Woodstock of '99!"

"What about it?" Brendolyn asks.

"We riot! Police will come if it gets out of control enough. They'll shut it down early. Before the finale," I explain with excitement of my brilliant plan.

"So you want us to commit a crime," she says to clarify.

"Yes."

Brendolyn takes a deep breath and sighs, “Alright. Let’s get this place shut the fuck down!”

We rage.

We start knocking over trash cans and rolling them into the crowd of angry moshers. They pick them up and throw them around. We knock over merch tables and squirt ketchup and mustard into the crowd. The crowd starts to catch on. They ransack the merch tents. I actually feel really bad about that. Someone climbs on top of the taco truck and starts banging his chest like King Kong. *Okay, that one identifies as Ape not wolf. Got it.*

The crow is angry, and destructive. The bands play on, ignoring the chaos in the crowd. We wait for them to realize what’s going on. We wait for the shut down. We wait for the cops. The shitters are literally lit on fire at this point, ready to launch like a rocket. It’s only a matter of time before security has had enough. We wait.

CHAPTER 25

Chapter Song

"Bark at the Moon" by Ozzy Osbourne

The longer we wait, the wilder the night gets. The whole place is destroyed by wolves and humans alike. Yet nothing. Not a single security officer or staff member seems phased. I know these things are expected at music festivals anymore, but one would think someone would shut it down.

"AHOOOOOOOOOOOOOO," the sound of a mighty werewolf echos from off stage. Everyone stops and turns their attention to their mighty leader.

Borris walks to center stage, mic in hand. The band that was playing stops and makes room for him. It's as if they're entranced.

"Ladies and gentlemen, now's the time you've all been waiting for. The moon is high, and shining bright tonight. The music is loud. If you came here human, be prepared to leave a full-blown werewolf!"

The crowd howls and cheers. They're either all dumb and think this is part of the act, or they're here for it. Borris continues on, "Are you ready?! Wolf Pack, Unite!"

The wolves all howl again. The band starts up playing loud and hard. The crowd goes wild for it. Everyone forgot about the riot, and are sucked into the music. Before our eyes more crowd members break out into the wolves that lie within them.

I put my ear plugs in, and look at Brendolyn. She has her ears covered. "If this doesn't work, and if

I don't make it out as human, Lena, you might be our only hope. You have to figure out how to save us! Save Melissa!"

"We're going to be fine! Quick, let's get away from the crowd. It's safer."

The music is getting louder and louder. The howls are like a choir singing backup. We run away from the crowd and head towards the camp where it's quieter. Our campsite is completely trashed. Everything. All the camps are ransacked. The music is still audible, but quieter at least.

BANG, BANG, BANG gun fire can be heard from the stage.

"And we thought a mass shooting was the only thing we'd have to worry about coming to this," Brendolyn mumbles while sitting on a log. I sit down next to her.

"I can see what all the fuss is about though, the moon is nice out," I say while looking up at the sky.

"Yeah, but it's strange. The full moon already passed," Brendolyn points out.

"Yeah, it looks pretty full to me," I say. The moon is wide and round, with a silver glow.

A flare flies up to the sky. I suspect maybe someone finally decided to call in the reinforcements. The flare flies high, it looks like it's almost as high as the moon.

CRACK The flare crashes into the moon. The moon shatters to pieces.

"What the hell just happened?!" I ask.

Brendolyn jaw is dropped, eye bugging wide, "I don't know, but there's moon matter raining down. We have to hide!"

We run. We don't know where to go. We don't know what's happening. Moon matter is pouring down from the sky in little shards of glass and tiny silver bullets. The dogs are crying, we can hear their whimpers and whines from the distance.

"We have to find Melissa!" Brendolyn says.

"We don't know where she is. She left us," I say. We cannot leave our hiding spot. It's too dangerous.

"Lena, she's our friend. We have to try!"

"Fuck. Alright, we're probably dead anyway. Let's go."

We get up and run back into the crowd of chaos, dodging dogs and moon debris left and right.

"The dogs are dying!" Brendolyn exclaims.

"What?!"

"Look! The ones that have been hit. They're dying. There must be something in the moon that's killing them."

I look around, beaten and bloodied dogs lie everywhere; gasping for air.

"Why would Borris want to turn everyone into wolves, just to kill them off?" I ask.

"I don't know. But it seems to be what's happening."

We keep running towards the back stage to try to find Melissa and hope she's still alive. And if she is, hope we can convince her to come with us.

The music is still playing loud. Brendolyn starts to scream. I look and realize she's not right next to me anymore. She stopped. She's covering her ears, but it's not working. *Fuck.*

This was too dangerous. We shouldn't have left the camp site.

I watch helplessly as my longest friend morphs into a monster. Hair sprouts out of her arms, legs, face, and neck. Her nose elongates into a snout, and her ears perk up like a dog's. She lets out a howl up at the crumbling moon. Her eyes widen, and she looks at me. Tears welled up in her eyes. I look at the sky and watch as massive chunks of moon crush her new wolf body.

I run after her, pulling the moon pieces off of her. It's hot, and searing the flesh off of my hands. Adrenaline is racing through my body. I feel no pain. I have to get the rock off of her. It's crushing her. It's so heavy. I can't move it by myself. I look around for anyone who can help. There's no one. Everyone is either a wolf, or dead wolf at this point. I look for anything to help me. A pole, or umbrella, anything. Nothing. So I run and ram into the boulder like

Bobby Boucher just heard someone say the water is bad. It budges. I keep pushing. It finally rolls over enough to get the weight off my friend.

I inspect her. She's not breathing. It looks like her lungs were crushed. Her head has a gash in it. I hug her beaten body tight, as tears fall down my face. I hold her lifeless body, while chaos continues to surround me.

"Look out!" I hear someone yell in my direction. I sit up to see what's going on. Moon matter continues to fall. I look down towards Brendolyn, and notice something shiny sticking out of her head wound. I carefully inspect it further. It looks like the silver shards that fell from the moon. It's getting brighter. I look around and notice the same thing is happening to all the wolves' heads. I panic and reach in and pull the piece of silver moon out of her head and throw it across the lawn. It was hot and sharp. And I'm glad I did!

The glowing pieces of moon keeps getting brighter and brighter and the band STILL PLAYS ON! Then it happens. Bursting brains! The moon got too hot and now everyone's heads are exploding. Disgusted, I find a trash can to hurl. This is all just too much right now. I give up on Melissa. She's long gone, and she and Borris are the reason for my best friend and all these innocent people's deaths. *Why am I still here?*

CHAPTER 26

Chapter Song

"Nightmare" by Avenged Sevenfold

I say my goodbyes to Brendolyn, and rage fills me to go find Melissa or Borris or both. I run to the backstage where I find the two of them lounging, laughing at the sight of horror and sipping out of jewel embellished challaces.

"What the actual fuck?!" I exclaim. I had no other words.

Borris stands up and laughs. "Oh, yeah sorry about your little friend there. I told you girls to stay away," Borris said all smug. Fucking jerk.

"Yeah, well now she's dead and it's your fault!"

"She could have been smart like me and allied with Borris," Melissa chimes in.

"Oh don't you even start!" I yell back at her.

"Look, doll. It'll be fine. It's just a mere revenge party. Survival of the fittest. Unfortunately, she wasn't the fittest. But don't you feel better knowing that now you're here with us, the true superior ones? It's natural selection baby, and we've won the lottery!"

Borris and Melissa howl in celebration.

"No! This is wrong! It's MURDER!"

"Well, murder or not, by the time anyone ever comes to find them, we will be long gone. And everyone will just assume it was another one of those crazed drugged out music festivals where everyone was too high to realize they got eaten by bears," Borris explained.

"You're wrong! I'm alive! And I'm a lawyer dammit! You're not getting away with this!"

Borris and Melissa laugh, "Good luck mailing your lawsuit to Hell, baby. Because that's where we live now. And as for you, that dream of yours was more of a nice foreshadow wasn't it? You're welcome."

"What do you mean you're welcome?" I ask.

"I planted that in your head. Why do you think I didn't wake you sooner? I wanted to see you see what lied ahead. You all alone, without anyone to help you. And if any of the wolves survive this moon blast, you sure as hell won't outrun them!" Borris steps in closer to me, "Now your nightmare's come to life."

I'm enraged and don't even know what to say. I look at Melissa. She smiles in my direction and waves, "You should have really listened to us sooner." And the two of them walk away; leaving me there to process what the hell they just said.

I turn around and see the horror scene of a battle ground in front of me. I'm terrified, broken, and sick to my stomach. I have no food. We destroyed it all. I lost my two closest friends. And I don't even know if I'm going to pack up and leave this place. Brendolyn had the car keys. Her body lies lifeless. But, at least her head didn't explode like all the others. That has to count for something. There has to be a way to bring her back. I look at her and vow, I WILL avenge her!

EPILOGUE

Chapter Song

"Dinosaur" by Theory of a Deadman

****Mood: Post-Apocalyptic****

I run to our campsite. I gather everything I can salvage left up, and I migrate to the woods. I am determined to figure this out. Brendolyn brought her hippy things with her; crystals, tarot, books on mythology and astrology. There has to be something in here to help me figure out how to save her.

I gather sticks, and reinforce the tent with a stronger shelter. It's disguised into the trees. I stay up for the remainder of the night reading, listening, plotting, and planning my next move.

Once it calmed down, and there was silence, I went back out. I kept my focus and ignored the bodies scattered around me. I went straight for Brendolyn's body. I wrapped it in a blanket for comfort, because even in her afterlife, she should be comfortable. Then I rolled her burrito onto a tarp. I drug that tarp all the way back to the tent, and lay her to rest next to my shelter. I know the decay will be putrid if I don't revive her soon enough. I guess that's my twisted way of reinforcing my motivation to get the job done…

TO BE CONTINUED.....

www.ingramcontent.com/pod-product-compliance
Lightning Source LLC
Chambersburg PA
CBHW060758310726
48980CB00002B/140

* 9 7 9 8 2 1 8 1 4 9 0 9 3 *